"How can you think I was making up to Esmée when I am in love with you?" he said angrily.

The declaration robbed her of argument. She looked shyly at him and said in a thrushlike voice her mama would have approved, "Are you really, Revel?"

"I must be. I can't eat; I can't sleep. I keep seeing you at Revel Hall, at the foot of my table, scolding me. It must be love."

"It sounds more like the megrims," she said doubtfully. Yet similar sensations had been bedeviling her, and she knew she was hopelessly in love with Revel.

"There is only one way to be sure," he said, pulling her into his arms. By the wan moonlight, he gazed at her upturned face a long moment before lowering his lips to kiss her.

WIFE
ERRANT

Joan Smith

FAWCETT CREST • NEW YORK

A Fawcett Crest Book
Published by Ballantine Books
Copyright © 1992 by Joan Smith

Library of Congress Catalog Card Number: 92-90612

ISBN 0-449-22015-X

Manufactured in the United States of America

First Edition: October 1992

Chapter One

"Tighter, Henshaw. Tighter. My waist used to be nineteen inches," Mrs. Marchant said, holding for dear life to the bedpost while her dresser pulled on the laces of her corset.

"You used to be nineteen years old, too, milady, but that was two decades ago. Why are you wearing this fitted gown?"

"Because Lord James is taking me to a costume ball, ninny, and I am going as a French lady of the eighteenth century."

"With your arms and shoulders bare?" Henshaw tsked.

"My face is reduced to a shambles," Mrs. Marchant said, but she said it with the complacent air of a rich man complaining of his expenses. "I must display my arms and shoulders if I hope to receive any compliments. Lord James told me I have arms like the *Venus de Milo*."

"The *Venus de Milo* does not have arms, Mama," her elder daughter pointed out. Both Mrs. Marchant's daughters were allowed to watch the grande toilette. It was their evening's sole entertainment.

"You must be sure to tell Lord James so, my dear," her mother said, with an angry glint. "I am sure all your gentlemen friends enjoy your little barbs quite as much as I do. Tighter, Henshaw. Tighter, I say."

"Stop, Henshaw! She is croaking!" Miss Marchant exclaimed.

The dame's face was indeed scarlet, but it was still distressingly beautiful. It was almost an embarrassment for a daughter to have a mother so much prettier than she was herself. Tess hardly knew which was more harmful: her mother's excess of beauty, or her total lack of discretion. No one would take Mrs. Marchant for thirty-nine to look at her. And to hear her, one would place her age closer to sixteen.

She still maintained the high-pitched, breathless voice of her youth, nor had her conversation improved with the years. Gowns and coiffures, parties and beaux had always been her main concerns. Now that her husband had left her, she entered into those maidenly interests with the vigor of desperation.

"That will do, Henshaw!" Mrs. Marchant squealed. "I am squeezed in like dressing in a turkey. Now let us see if we can get the gown done up."

Mrs. Marchant held her breath while the faithful Henshaw fastened the buttons on an elaborate confection of blue silk with wide panniers. When the closing was achieved, she looked very bizarre and very lovely. The gown displayed not only a tiny waist but a generous expanse of bosom. Her contemporary English coiffure lent an anachronistic touch to the ensemble, like a bishop in full regalia, but minus his miter. Her tousle of blond curls was dressed in the latest vogue, held in place with a silver ribbon. Long kidskin gloves were added, to further confuse the toilette.

"You look beautiful, Mama." Miss Dulcie sighed, gazing rapturously.

"You should wear a white wig," Tess suggested.

"If you are referring to those three white hairs that had sprung out at my temples, you need not worry, Tess. I yanked them out." She patted her curls and made a moue in the mirror. "Thank God I am a blonde. I cannot think anyone spotted them."

"Actually I was referring to your French period costume."

Mrs. Marchant ignored this, as she usually ignored her elder daughter's advice on matters of toilette. The peacock did not go to the sparrow for advice on feathers. She stood back to survey herself in the cheval glass. A petulant smile settled on her lips as she turned this way and that, admiring her fulsome figure. Her husband may have abandoned her, but no one could say it was because she had let herself go. She had never been in better looks than she was at nine and thirty. Were it not for the girls, she could pass for a decade younger, whereas her lord and master, Mr. Lyle Marchant, looked every one of his fifty years.

What was the matter with gentlemen, that they could never keep their hands off the younger ladies? Lyle's current flirt, a dashing widow named Esmée Gardener, *claimed* to be half Lyle's age. Liar! It was really too bad of him to have taken up with her. This holiday at Bath was to have been a second honeymoon, although a honeymoon encumbered with two grown daughters was hardly likely to fan the flames of a moribund passion. She had sat still for a series of Lyle's amours at home at Northbay, but Bath was different.

It was at Bath twenty-two years before that she

3

and Lyle had met and fallen in love. Bath was special to her, almost a shrine. But the first week they were here, he had clapped eyes on Esmée, and that was the end of the honeymoon. He was after her like a hound after a hart. Well, she had showed him this time. She had put his trunks on the doorstep, had had the locks changed, and had informed her lawyer to serve Mr. Marchant with divorce papers.

Her lawyer, a Mr. Pargeter, had not been at all helpful. He had suggested an ecclesiastical divorce, *a mensa et thoro*—whatever *that* might be—should be obtained first, after which an Act of Parliament appeared to be necessary. Parliament was getting a good deal too big for its breeches when it invaded a lady's private life. To add to her difficulties, Pargeter seemed very unsure that Lyle's having a mistress entitled her to a divorce, whereas if *she* had a lover, Lyle might turn her off with less difficulty. She had prevailed upon Pargeter to send Lyle a letter hinting at divorce, and meanwhile instituted a case of legal separation.

Pargeter was very insistent that she keep the children. Northbay, the fine estate in Wiltshire where she and Lyle lived, was *her* parental home. Her papa had wisely entailed it on their son, Henry, who was at Harrow, so she would not have to leave Northbay. That would make Lyle sit up and take notice! He was very proud of Northbay; it was a finer estate than his own place in York. Ha! Wouldn't he hate to have to remove to the Briars! That would bring him crawling back to her.

She shook these old worries from her mind and smiled brightly on her audience. "I am off, my dears," she said, placing a kiss on her youngest, Dulcie—the image of herself and her favorite. She

4

brushed cheeks with her elder daughter, Tess. Tess favored Lyle in looks, with her crow black hair and serious gray eyes and critical expression.

"What shall we say if Papa comes?" Tess enquired brusquely.

"He won't, but if he does, be sure to tell him I am out with Lord James Drake. As it is a private party, he won't be able to bring his *chère amie*."

"Pity," Tess said. "I fancy Esmée would feel right at home at any party the raffish Lord James is invited to. If you *must* act like a loose woman, Mama, I wish you had not come to Bath. Bath is the most straitlaced city in England."

"Gudgeon. No one goes to London in the dead of winter. But I shall go in the spring and present Dulcie."

She was out the door on a flutter of fingers, leaving the shambles of her tempestuous toilette behind her. Gowns and petticoats and shawls littered the bed. As to the toilette table, it looked as if a cyclone had hit it.

"Why is she *doing* this?" Dulcie howled. "A divorced lady cannot present a daughter at court."

"She should know better at her age," Tess agreed.

"Woosha," Henshaw said, picking up loose hairpins from the powdered top of the dressing table. "It is her age that drives her to it. It isn't easy turning forty. She fears she is losing her looks—and her husband." The homely Henshaw had never had either of these items to lose, and did not regret it. Living vicariously through her mistress was excitement enough.

"I think she looks as lovely as ever," Dulcie said.

"So she does," Henshaw agreed, "but it takes two hours to put her in looks now. We used to accomplish it inside of an hour."

"In her fortieth year, she ought to be cultivating her mind, not her face," Tess said.

"When did Papa ever care for a lady's mind?" Dulcie countered.

"He never did, and neither does any other gentleman, so far as I know," Tess replied blandly.

"It's not fair," Dulcie said, sulking. "You and I must sit home because we have no one to take us to the Assembly Rooms."

"We could not go in any case. How could we be seen in public when the word *divorce* is being whispered about?"

"Mama is not such a flat as that!" Dulcie said. "She has not told anyone, and she does not let Lord James take her to public do's. She only sent the letter to try to frighten Papa into returning. What she ought to have done is speak to Lady Revel. Lord James Drake is her cousin, you must know. The Revels are here in Bath."

Tess looked interested in this notion. While the Dowager Countess of Revel was a neighbor, the families were not close socially. Tess was only at Revel Hall on public days, or occasionally on the vicar's behalf to beg for charity. She met the countess at church, or in the village. Lady Revel seemed a good-natured dame, but not one to bestir herself for mere social causes. Perhaps her son would be more useful. "Or Lord Revel," Tess said pensively. "He is a man of the world. He could explain to Lord James that he is behaving badly."

"Revel could hardly complain about that!" Dulcie said, and laughed. "He is a horrid flirt . . . but very handsome."

"He is a rake, but he has lofty views on propri-

6

ety. He never carries on with married ladies or debs. Only lightskirts and widows."

"But he is much younger than Lord James. Why would his cousin listen to him?"

"Because Lord Revel is top of the trees, and Lord James is only a lower twig," Tess replied. "Revel could impede Lord James's social life, if he cared to put himself to the bother. I shall call on Lady Revel tomorrow morning, and try for a word with Revel as well."

"Will you really? You are up to anything, Tess. I don't know how you can be so brave."

"Nonsense, what has bravery to do with it?" Tess asked, but she did feel a tremble of apprehension. As she studied her sister's enchanting face, she felt it might find more success with Lord Revel than her own lesser charms. She felt instinctively that the way to get at him was through a pretty face. "Will you come with me, Dulcie?"

"Mama has asked the coiffeur to call tomorrow morning. I mean to have my hair cut à la cheribime."

"First things first, child. We shan't be going out to show off our coiffures unless we manage to get Mama and Papa back together."

"We can always go for rides and walks at least."

Henshaw shoo'd them out of the room, and the girls went belowstairs in the vain hope that some callers would come to enliven their dull evening.

"We must do something to bring Papa back," Dulcie said, thumbing a fashion magazine. "At least until I have had my Season."

"That sounds very selfish, Dulcie," Tess said. "You always think of yourself."

"So do they," Dulcie pointed out. "And it is your fault, Tess."

7

"My fault?" Tess gasped. "Upon my word, you have a lot of gall saying that. If it were not for me, Northbay would be in ruins."

"Exactly. You do all Mama's work for her. You even chaperone me, as often as not. Mama knows you keep an eye on things, so she can go on acting the carefree girl."

"Talk about ingratitude!"

"Oh, I am very grateful—that you have turned Mama into a selfish beast," Dulcie said, and flounced out of the saloon.

Tess sat on in stunned silence. Was this her thanks for doing her duty? Someone had to keep an eye on things at Northbay. And an eye on Dulcie, too. The girl had no more notion of propriety than a monkey. Less, and Mama never scolded her.

Tess rose to stride angrily from the room. As she passed the mirror, she caught her reflection staring back at her. That tightly controlled face reminded her of someone . . . Who was it? She had seen that air of long-suffering somewhere recently. It flashed suddenly into her mind. Saint Jerome, in the stained-glass window in the church at home, being lashed and bearing it stoically. The curate had told her it was only a dream Saint Jerome had, although the saint went on to live a life of fasting in the desert, or some such heroic thing. If not a martyr, he was certainly a saint.

Was that how Dulcie saw her? Saints, it seemed, received no gratitude in this world. Dulcie was the favorite of both her mama and papa. It was Dulcie who was to have the Season. There had been some talk of giving herself one when she was eighteen, but she had not raised a single whimper when the idea was abandoned. "Money is a little tight this year,

Tess," her father had said. "We'll take you next year." Then he bought himself a new carriage and team. Next year Mama had had a miscarriage, and the year after that, Tess was suddenly too old to make the trip worthwhile. "You would feel a quiz at your age, with all the young debs," Mama had said.

Tess went up to her room to brush her hair, vaguely disturbed by her undutiful reflections. But she was right, for all her sense of guilt. Dulcie had said her parents always thought of themselves, and she was right, too, although she ought not to have said it. "It is your fault." That was her thanks for being a dutiful daughter and sister. Was Dulcie right about that, too? Had her taking charge turned her parents into these pattern cards of selfishness? No, they were both bone selfish to begin with; she had just made it easier for them to stave off disaster. But disaster had nearly caught up with them this time, despite her efforts.

Why had she let everyone walk all over her? Lacking Mama's and Dulcie's beauty, she had tried to curry favor by being the sensible, reliable one. "Tess will take care of it. You can always count on Tess." But deep in their hearts, they resented her hold on the reins.

Perhaps it was time for a change. The ascetic face in the mirror took on a sly smile as the brush slid through her black, silky hair. Henshaw, she knew, would be preparing Dulcie for bed. Tess always looked after herself. She saw the shadow of Saint Jerome's self-righteous expression and frowned. Really, there was something unattractive about those priggish, self-righteous women. Papa's idea of an insult to a lady was to call her a Hannah More, and there was a streak of the do-gooder Hannah in Tess.

She had given her youth to her mother, and her thanks was that Mama preferred Dulcie. Everyone preferred Dulcie, with her golden curls and her easy smile. Tess studied the face in the mirror and thought it could be quite as attractive as Dulcie's, if it received the same amount of care. Her eyes, though gray, were as large and lustrous as Dulcie's. The four years difference in their ages was not sufficient to make Tess old. Maturity had settled on her at a young age, but she was not old.

She just acted old, while her mama played the young flirt. Would Mama change if she had no one at home to do her worrying for her? She had still some inkling of propriety, for she was at pains to keep her plans for a divorce quiet, in hopes that Papa would repent. Mama did not mind being called a dasher—she gloried in it—but she would not want to be put truly beyond the social pale. Society was her life. It was time for her mama to grow up, and that could only be accomplished by brute force. Tess would try to gain Lord Revel's help in restraining Lord James as well. Without the distraction of this high flyer, Mama would have more time to worry about her elder daughter.

It was Tess's custom to go to Dulcie's room before she retired, to see if her young sister was settled in for the night. She undressed and turned down her counterpane. Her face still wore a sly smile as she climbed between the sheets without visiting Dulcie. It was the first tentative step in her campaign to reform her family. Now she had to consider what larger steps must be taken.

Chapter Two

"You forgot to come to my room last night, Tess," Dulcie said when she came to breakfast the next morning. "I especially wanted to talk to you. I was feeling so very blue about Mama and Papa, I cried myself to sleep," she said, casting an accusing look at Tess.

"When you flounced out of the saloon, I took the idea you did not wish to speak to me," Tess replied blandly.

"It was Mama I was angry with."

"Then you ought not to have taken it out on me."

A small lecture from Tess was nothing new. Dulcie paid it little heed. They were soon joined by their mama, whose pale cheeks and smudged eyes rendered her less lovely than the night before. She had not yet had a session at her toilette with the formidable Henshaw. She said good morning to her daughters and looked about the table for her mail.

"Have you handled the correspondence already, Tess?" she asked. "You might at least have left the invitations for me to read."

"I have not done the correspondence, Mama. I slept in this morning," Tess replied.

"There is no hurry. You can do it after breakfast."

"Mama!" Dulcie objected. "Tess is taking me to Milsom Street this morning."

"Bother! As you are going out, pick me up some headache powders and my shoes—they are at the cobbler's. I wrenched the heel loose. You can do the correspondence this afternoon."

"Actually, I plan to go out this afternoon as well," Tess said. "To visit Lady Revel."

"I suppose we ought to pay our respects, not that she will return the call."

"Then you will be coming with me?" Tess asked innocently.

"You know perfectly well I have the coiffeur coming," Mrs. Marchant snipped. "You ought to do something about your own looks, Tess. You never spend a penny in that direction, and it shows, my dear." Tess looked interested in this idea. She had decided she required a gentleman for optimum misbehavior, and obviously a new hairdo would be required.

When her mother saw her hesitation, she rushed on. "You must pay my respects to Lady Revel. You will know what to say, and don't tell her why I am staying at home. Keep your ears open for any mention of Lord James. I fear he is seeing another lady. He scarcely threw me a word all evening, and brought me home very early. His friends are all such rattles they have no idea of flirtation."

"I did not hear you come home, Mama," Tess said, "and I was awake till midnight, reading."

"Midnight is early, goose. I don't doubt he went on somewhere else after. The man is an eel. The masquerade was a dead bore. All the ladies were dressed in Oriental garb, thanks to Lord Byron. I was the only lady there without a black wig."

12

Tess soon excused herself from the table.

Her mother said, "Don't forget to look at the mail. There is bound to be something from Northbay needing a reply."

"I shall have Crimshaw bring the mail to you."

"Only the invitations. You can handle the housekeeper's correspondence."

"I am so busy today, Mama, I fear you will have to do it yourself," Tess said.

"You call gadding about Milsom Street busy?"

"Shall I stay home and do the correspondence then?"

Dulcie set up a wail, and Mrs. Marchant decided the correspondence could wait till the evening.

The morning on busy Milsom Street with Dulcie was uneventful. With a thought to the new role she was about to undertake, Tess bought a few additions to her toilette, the most noteworthy of which was a new bonnet with an arched rim to frame her face and a clutch of ostrich feathers dyed pink. She "forgot" the slippers at the cobbler's, but bought the headache powders, as Mama would have ample need for them.

Mrs. Marchant was quite taken with the bonnet when she clamped her eyes on it. "How exceedingly stylish!" she exclaimed. "Not in your usual mode, Tess. I must have one like it. But you will not want to appear in a bonnet like your mama's." She laughed gaily. "You can buy one similar, with a different color of feather." As she spoke, she took the bonnet to the mirror and arranged it on her head.

Tess's first reaction was pleasure that for once she had chosen something that pleased her mama. Her instinct was to hand the bonnet over, but a

13

second thought told her this was the behavior of a martyr. "Don't you think pink just a trifle lively for an older lady, Mama?"

Her mother blinked in astonishment. The greater crime was not refusing to hand over the bonnet, but using the word "older." Mrs. Marchant was accustomed to being taken for Tess's sister. Tess took the bonnet and left, with an awful feeling of betrayal in her breast.

"What ails that girl?" Mrs. Marchant complained to Dulcie. "I swear she becomes more selfish by the day. Older lady indeed! Where did she buy the bonnet?"

"At Madame Jardin's, on Milsom Street, Mama."

"I shall dash out this afternoon. Bother! We have the coiffeur coming. Get the fashion magazines, Dulcie, and let us choose our new hairstyles."

After lunch, Tess put on her new bonnet to call on Lady Revel, but it was Lord Revel's admiration she was looking for. He was the reigning buck of the county at home. She never had any hope—or even any wish—of attaching such a high flyer. In fact she heartily disapproved of his life-style, but like any maiden, she wanted to look her best in front of him.

The Revels were staying in an absent relative's house on the elegant Royal Crescent. The Marchants had hired a smaller house on Bartlett Street, midway between their two most favored destinations, the Assembly Rooms and Milsom Street. As she was driven along, Tess had ample opportunity to admire the Palladian architecture of the famous Woods, *père* and *fils*, who had done much of the building in Bath. The town spread out below her in

14

tiers of terraces, squares, and crescents, the whole bound around by the Avon.

Lady Revel held no real terrors for Tess. Despite her title and wealth, she was a plain-looking and plain-spoken country lady. She had lost any interest in her appearance after she had nabbed a husband. Her hair had silvered, and her pale cheeks were always innocent of rouge. It was unlikely that she would be out, or that she would be entertaining company. She came annually to Bath for the waters, declaring, "Anything that tastes this wretched has to be good for you." Her complaint was rheumatism, which used to bite at her elbows and neck, but had unaccountably flown to her ankles and toes this year.

Tess found the dame alone before a blazing grate, in a faded gown of blue serge, reading a novel by Fanny Burney and sipping tea.

"Tess!" she exclaimed. "Aren't you the Good Samaritan, to visit an old ruin like me. Come and tell me all the *on-dits*. Anthony never tells me anything. Nothing he does is fit to tell, I wager. I daresay he has a new dasher. Have you heard anything about her?"

Tess took up her seat on the sofa and was handed a cup of tea. "Thank you. No, indeed, Lady Revel. I have not heard he has a ladybird under his protection."

"I don't *know* that he has, but Figgs tells me he has broken up with his latest one. She was a widow called Esmée, whom, James tells me, is accepted in the less distinguished homes. James would know about less distinguished homes," she added acidly. "A Flanders mare, in other words. I never trust a woman who calls herself Esmée. It has a whiff of

15

the theater. I wager she was an actress. Lightskirts ought not to make claims to respectability. I much prefer a simple trollop to one who puts on airs."

"Esmée! You cannot mean Mrs. Gardener!"

"Why, yes, I believe that was the name. Why do you stare, child? Is she a gazetted horror? Is she likely to burden us with a paternity suit, or publish her memoirs?"

"Esmée Gardener is the woman Papa—"

"You never mean it!" the countess exclaimed, clapping her knee in derision. "I had not heard your papa was on the prowl again. The female has catholic tastes. Good God! I wonder if Anthony knows this. How he will hoot to hear it."

"It is about Esmée and Papa—and Mama—that I have come, Lady Revel."

The dame patted Tess's hand and tsked. "It will pass, my dear. Your papa is always taken by a new petticoat, but he soon tires of them and comes home with his tail between his legs. I never paid any heed to my husband's flirts. I welcomed the respite."

"This time it is different," Tess said. "Mama is carrying on with a gentleman as well."

Lady Revel listened and nodded. "Good for her. I don't see why a wronged wife ought not to enjoy a few discreet delinquencies, if she has a taste for it. A handsome widower, I wager? A widower will always work his way with older ladies."

"No, he is not a widower. Mama says she will divorce Papa, and with Dulcie about to make her bows next spring, the scandal will be horrid. Indeed people are already whispering, Lady Revel. Dulcie and I have not been to a single assembly or party since Mama began going about with this gentleman."

"Selfish creature! She and Lyle are from the same

16

basket. But the divorce is only a threat, depend upon it. Louise Marchant has always been a pea-goose, but she is not fool enough to try to divorce her husband. Who is the scoundrel she is seeing?"

"It's Lord James Drake. That is why I came to you, hoping you would speak to him."

Lady Revel drew a long, exasperated sigh. "I might have guessed! They were rolling their eyes at each other when he visited me last summer. The devil of it is, James never pays any heed to me. He would cut up all the harder to spite me. He was the baby of the family, you must know, and was always spoiled rotten." She furrowed her brow in thought and said, "Who he might listen to is Anthony. There is no point talking morality to James, but if he could be convinced it is bad ton, he would desist."

"Is Lord Revel at home?" Tess asked as calmly as she could. She felt a nervous churning to ask for an interview with Revel. She was by no means on those same easy terms with him as with his mama. He spent considerably less time at Revel Hall, and when he was there, he usually brought his company with him. Revel was not such a high stickler that he avoided the local do's, at which he was sure to stand up with his neighbor, but the Marchants were not invited to his private parties.

"I didn't see him go out. I'll ask Figgs." She hollered into the hall, as the bell cord required rising from her comfortable sofa.

A butler who looked strangely like a bulldog in a jacket appeared at the doorway. "You screeched, your ladyship?"

Lady Revel explained to her guest, "I owe Figgs a guinea. He beat me roundly at faro last night, and is feeling full of himself." She turned to Figgs, "No, Master Jackanapes, I did not screech. I hollered. Send Lord Revel to me."

"His lordship is in the bath, madam. And it was a guinea and tuppence. You promised a tuppence for the use of my cards."

"You never pay *me* tuppence when we use *my* cards. Haul Anthony out and send him down."

"His lordship dislikes to be interrupted at the bath."

"This is a matter of urgency, Figgs. And bring us some fresh tea. Bohea, mind. This tastes like dishwater."

Figgs picked up the tray and marched from the room. "Figgs might possibly be my cousin Gerald's by-blow," Lady Revel explained. "This is Gerald Drake's house we are using, while Gerald is in London. Figgs was landed on Gerald as a babe. Gerald never knew quite what to do with him. I do not see any trace of the Drakes in him. I believe he was foisted on my cousin in error, or by design. In any case, he is a good cardplayer, but a wretched butler."

They chatted about Bath doings until the tea arrived, and close behind it came Lord Revel, wearing a navy flannel dressing gown with a white towel around his neck. His wet hair was all askew, and his feet encased in slippers knitted by his mama.

"Anthony!" his mama exclaimed. "Good God, is this any way to appear in public? There is a lady present! Did Figgs not tell you?"

"Figgs used the word 'Urgent!' I thought you had set the house afire at least." He turned to Tess. "My apologies, Miss Marchant. I shall return presently." He bowed and left, chewing a smile. It had

18

been worth the embarrassment to see Tess Marchant's eyes trotting all over him as if she'd never seen a man not fully clothed before. Very likely she hadn't, come to that. Her chronic rectitude annoyed him. He knew he ought to admire her many sterling qualities, but frankly, he preferred a little naughtiness in his ladies.

Lady Revel explained, "I am a virtual hermit here. I so seldom have any callers that Anthony doesn't care how he walks around the house, but he does not usually come downstairs without his trousers on at least."

Tess blushed like a blue cow and said it did not matter in the least. But she knew that when Revel returned, it was she would be ill at ease with the memory of that glimpse of bare chest, with the patch of black hair showing above the dressing gown.

Chapter Three

Some half hour passed; the tea chilled in the pot, and still Lord Revel did not come. Lady Revel was threatening to hobble upstairs after him herself when the sound of languid footsteps heralded his approach. Tess looked to the doorway and felt the wait was well worth it. Lord Revel, fresh from his toilette, was a very pineapple of perfection.

It was generally agreed, among the few hundred gentlemen who cared for such things, that no figure became Weston's jackets so well as Lord Revel's broad shoulders and tapering torso. His cravat was a marvel of pristine intricacy; his biscuit-colored trousers free of either wrinkle or spot; and his Hessians gleamed like black diamonds. His closely cropped hair was brushed forward à la Titus, lending a rakish air to the severity of a straight nose and angular jaw. His lean face was bronzed from riding, and wore such an expression of ennui that one would think he had lived a hundred full lives. Eyes of an unholy blue twinkled mischievously, to belie his air of studied indifference.

He glided forward, performed an exquisite bow, and said, "A thousand pardons, Miss Marchant. I shall have Figgs thrashed for his dereliction."

Tess had collected herself, and betrayed not a jot

of the turmoil she was feeling. "One pardon will do, Lord Revel. I am sure a thrashing is not necessary."

"Nor possible," Lady Revel added. "Figgs could darken your daylights, Anthony. Now sit down and stop making a cake of yourself. There is no need to put on airs. It is only Tess Marchant."

"Only?" he exclaimed, annoyed at his audience's cavalier treatment. Miss Marchant ought to be close to swooning by now. He would turn up the charm. "Really, Mama. One does not use 'only' in the same sentence as 'Miss Marchant.' " He took up a seat on the striped sofa and gracefully threw one leg over the other. "About Figgs's claim of urgency: How much do you need this time, Miss Marchant? Are we providing coats or candles?"

"I am not taking subscriptions today, Lord Revel," she said. "I only do that at home, for the church, you know, or the orphanage."

"Money is not *urgent*, Anthony," his mama said.

"That depends very much on the circumstances. But I scent a more interesting story here. Pray proceed, Miss Marchant." He turned the full blaze of his sapphire orbs on her and smiled his encouragement.

Before Tess was seduced into admiration, he immediately helped himself to a cup of tea and complained that there were no sandwiches.

"Figgs can bring you some cucumber sandwiches, if you like," his mama offered.

"Where do you get cucumbers at this time of year?" Tess asked.

"Figgs can get anything," Lady Revel said categorically.

Lord Revel declined the offer of a sandwich and turned expectantly to Tess, mildly curious to hear

21

what had brought her. Tess took a deep breath and considered how to phrase her request.

Impatient, Revel said, "It is Dulcie. Such charming young ladies inevitably fall into a hobble with the gentlemen. Only give me his name and I shall undertake to call him out."

"No, it is not that bad, Lord Revel. And it is not Dulcie. It is Mama."

"Ah, the other Marchant charmer. But surely your mama has a more likely defender. I refer, of course, to your father."

Revel was so busy being clever that he failed to notice for a moment that he had unintentionally slighted his caller. To imply that this dull lump of a lady was one whit less charming than her mother was, no doubt, wounding. He smiled easily and added, "They have wisely sent the most charming of the lot to seek my help. What can I do for you, Miss Marchant?"

His mother said, "You can stop playing off your airs and graces, gudgeon, and listen. Your cousin James is carrying on with Louise. You must speak to him."

"Surely your cousin lands in *your* bailiwick, Mama," he said, subtly shifting the onus of the relationship to buttress his position.

"Much attention James would pay to me."

"Or to me. Indeed there is some irony in such a tarnished vessel as I calling uncle black."

"I am not so foolish as to expect you to preach propriety," his mother said bluntly. "What you must tell him is that it is bad ton to take advantage of a married lady."

"Mmmm. Especially when her *esposo* is so close to hand, and not a bad shot, either. That is rather raffish of James."

22

"Then tell him so."

"He surely knows it."

"Yes, but he does not know that Mama is planning to get a divorce," Tess said.

"Divorce!" he exclaimed, shocked out of his lethargy. "Surely it would be wise to investigate less . . . questionable options before speaking of divorce!"

"Yes," Tess agreed, "but you know Mama has a taste for being a dasher. She does not realize the consequences to others."

"Nor to herself," he added. "Propriety apart, the thing will not succeed. A lady will never be given a divorce on such paltry grounds as adultery."

"Paltry!" Tess exclaimed, skewering him with a gimlet gaze.

Revel refused to be subjugated by mere morality. "Adultery is paltry in comparison with divorce," he insisted.

"Use your wits," his mama declared. "It is Mr. Marchant who will end up demanding a divorce, and it is James whose reputation will be sullied as partner in the crim. con."

"It would, of course, be a great pity to cast a stain on James's immaculate reputation," Revel said ironically, then he subsided into silence, with his eyes closed. Tess thought he had fallen asleep and wanted to strike him.

Before she succumbed to the urge, his eyes opened and he said, "You're right, Mama. It is Mr. Marchant who could hope to win a divorce, but it is Mrs. Marchant who owns Northbay, if memory serves. He will think twice before putting such a fine property at risk. James, on the other hand, is probably working under the misapprehension that Northbay belongs to Mrs. Marchant outright."

"Oh, no. It is entailed on Henry," Tess said.

"I wager James don't know that. If the threat of being blackened with a crim. con. don't provide a large enough stick to beat him into propriety, Northbay's being entailed will. Consider it done."

"I knew you would think of something, Lady Revel," Tess said. "Thank you so much."

Revel looked surprised that the thanks were not delivered to himself. He was too well-bred to display his surprise, and spoke of other things. "I expect you have been to take the waters at the Pump Room, Miss Marchant," he said, choosing the outing he thought would suit her.

"We tried the water once, but since then Dulcie and I just promenade to watch the people."

"I go faithfully every morning," Lady Revel said. "I just sit like a lump in the lounge. Promenading is impossible with this demmed toe. It aches worse than a bad tooth."

"If thy toe scandalize thee, cut it off," Revel suggested.

"Don't think I have not thought of it. The gout would only fly to my knee or my neck," she said resignedly.

Their conversation was interrupted by Figgs, who appeared at the doorway and announced, "He's here—Lord James." He turned to Revel and added, "Now is your chance to have a word with him."

Tess expected Lord Revel to cut up stiff at this breach of butlering etiquette. He gave a lazy smile and said, "Congratulations, Figgs. Your hearing has improved since you failed to hear my request for brandy last evening. I waited half an hour for it, and finally had to fetch it myself."

"The exercise is good for you. Keeps you soople," Figgs replied.

"Kind of you to be concerned for my health. Show Lord James into the study. I shall speak to him there."

Revel took his leave of the ladies. Tess began to gather up her gloves and reticule. "Wait a moment," Lady Revel said. "James won't stay long. He dislikes to be scolded. You may as well hear what Anthony has to say when he returns."

Within ten minutes, both gentlemen returned to the saloon. Lord James did not look chastened. His manner toward Tess was a little friendlier than before, which she took for a sign of compliance.

"Miss Marchant. Don't you look dashing this morning? A lovely bonnet," he said, touching the pink feathers.

Drake was a sort of blurred copy of Lord Revel. He was a decade and a half older, with the accompanying signs of age and dissipation. His hair was touched with silver at the temples, his brow was creased, and his manner just a shade too oily to please the discerning. Decades of having to cater to his betters had left their indelible mark. His eyes, in particular, lacked that devilish luster of Revel's. There was a sort of sly look in them, an insincerity.

"Thank you, Lord James. I just bought it this morning."

"You ought to be paid to wear it. You are a splendid advertisement for the milliner."

Lord Revel looked from James to Tess, to see how she reacted to this blatant flattery. She said, "Thank you," in cool accents. What a cold wench she was. Butter would freeze solid in her mouth.

"How is your bellyache, James?" Lady Revel

asked, to bring him down to earth. "The last time I saw you, you were suffering from cramps."

"A slight and passing indisposition, cousin. How's the toe?"

"Wretched."

They chatted for ten minutes, at which time Tess began to make her adieux, as Revel could hardly say anything interesting in front of his cousin.

"Not leaving so soon!" Lord James exclaimed.

"I have some letters to write," she said.

"Oh, letters! I never write letters," James said.

"You are being obtuse, cousin," Revel said, tossing a smile at Tess. "When a lady claims she must write some letters, it is a polite way of saying she is tired of the company. May I accompany you home, Miss Marchant?" He expected to see a flash of triumph in those stormy gray eyes. Nothing.

"My carriage is waiting," she said. "And I really do have to write letters. There was one from the bailiff."

"Ah, yes," Revel said, with a sapient glance at Lord James. "Northbay belongs to your mama, of course, until Henry takes control, so she will tell you what to write." That won him a small smile of approval.

"Mama takes very little interest. And with Papa so busy, I usually handle the correspondence myself. I daresay the bailiff is just pestering us to tile the west pasture again."

The gentlemen rose with Miss Marchant. Lord James said, "I wonder if I might impose on your kindness to give me a lift to Milsom Street, Miss Marchant? My rig is hors de combat. I tore a wheel loose in a race yesterday. These hills around Bath!"

"Did you win the race?" Revel asked.

"No, Anthony, I did not. I lost the wheel early in the game. But the betting was light." He turned back to Tess. "Miss Marchant?"

"Certainly, I will be happy to give you a ride, Lord James," she lied, and went out with him, her heart aflutter to be alone with her mama's beau.

In the saloon, Lady Revel said to her son, "What did you say to him?"

"Just what we discussed. He had no idea Northbay was entailed."

"But he will stop seeing her? Those poor girls are kept home every night, Anthony. They cannot go to the assemblies without a chaperone, and you may be sure James does not take the mama there."

"He says he has already made a few assignments with Mrs. Marchant. He will fulfill them—it would be rude to do otherwise—but he will cut the friendship off gently."

"Good. Now call Figgs. And give me some money. I owe him a guinea. Best make it two. He always wins. I am quite certain he cheats."

"I must show you how to palm the cards." Revel dropped some coins into his mother's outstretched palm and went to call Figgs.

In the Marchant's carriage, Lord James was walking on eggs. Anthony's announcement that Mrs. Marchant had a son was a sore blow. The boy had been at school when he met her, and she was not the sort of lady who harped on her children when she was with a gentleman. He thought Northbay was hers outright. An estate entailed on a son was no good to him. Tess, on the other hand, had a dot of ten thousand clear. Dulcie had the same, and she was prettier, but a lady close to a third his own age was just a trifle absurd. He was absurd enough without that. Tess was not much less than half his age.

"I want to apologize for my thoughtlessness, Miss Marchant," he said humbly. "I assure you my only motive in seeing your mama was to give her whatever solace my presence provided at this cruel time."

"Thank you, Lord James," she said, and was suddenly seized with a shaft of pity for the man. It was a shabby way to have to live, running from pillar to post. "I made sure you would see common sense when you knew the whole."

"I am such a selfish beast! I never gave a thought to you two girls, left alone night after night. My only thought was for your mama."

"It is Dulcie's debut next spring that is of particular concern, you see," she explained. "She could not be presented if Mama was divorced."

"And what of Miss Marchant's debut?" he asked archly. "I do not recall having seen you in London, ma'am. I am sure I would have noticed."

"I did not make my bows."

"So you two ladies will be presented together? What a treat for the gentlemen!"

"No, indeed! I would stay at Northbay to look after things."

"It is as I feared," he said. "You have already made your choice." Tess's pity began to fade. The old fool was taking a run at her ten thousand.

"No, it is not that. Mama was ill when I should have made my bows. Now I am a little old to be making a debut."

"Old! This is nonsense. You cannot be a day older than nineteen." He scrutinized her face for signs of age.

"I am going on twenty-two, Lord James."

Lord James garnered up all these details with

great glee. A fair-looking spinster firmly glued to the shelf; she would not balk at his age and lack of funds. A pity he had become entangled with the mama, but he might turn that to advantage, if he played his cards wisely.

"What a beautiful day it is!" he exclaimed, peering through the window. "Must you really dash home and write letters?"

"I am afraid I must." She had firmly decided she would not write those letters, but they provided an excuse to escape Lord James.

"Could we not take just a little spin into the countryside? I miss my poor old rig. Let me show you the route of the race I spoke of. It is not far. Just west of the Sydney Gardens. Have you seen the Sydney Gardens?"

"We more usually go to the Crescent Gardens, closer to home."

"You must see the Sydney Gardens. They used to be called the Vauxhall of Bath. What gay revels we—my papa enjoyed there, in the last century. I should very much like to show them to you."

Tess's besetting fault was that she found it hard to say no. Before she knew what was happening, Lord James had pulled the check string and directed the groom to Sydney Gardens. He beguiled the trip with a deal of flirtatious nonsense that set her teeth on edge. She reminded him of that famous beauty, Georgiana, Duchess of Devonshire; something about the way she spoke, and those killing eyes. Did she ride? Ah, she had not brought her mount, but he was sure a friend of his could provide one.

Eventually the carriage drove into the shady gardens, where more Bath chairs than pedestrians were to be seen at this haunt of the valetudinarian. Lord

James's power of invention was hard-pressed to find compliments on a winter garden bereft of blooms, but heavily littered with dank yews. They descended and strolled among the yews, until Tess said she found the wind chilly, and she really must be going.

"I have frozen you to the bone with my selfishness. You must let me give you a tea, Miss Marchant."

"That is not necessary, Lord James. I can have tea at home."

"But it is past teatime. There is a quaint little tea shop just south of the garden, on New Sydney Place. No argument. You would not make an old bachelor take his tea alone," he said, making a long face.

She was rushed along to a tea shop that purveyed an indifferent tea of Bath cakes and Bath buns, both stale. "Now I really must be going home," she said. The sun was already sinking low in these short winter days. "Mama will wonder what has happened to me."

"Shall I go in and make your apologies?" he suggested.

"I wish you would not," she said, her patience straining to remain civil. How could Mama stand the man?

Lord James would not hear of her dropping him off at his rooms, but sat in the carriage until she reached Bartlett Street. He did not insist on entering the house with her, however.

Tess was in a thoroughly cross mood by the time she got home. Crimshaw gave a shake of his bald head and said, "The mistress is waiting for you in the saloon, Miss Marchant. In a bit of a pelter," he added, to warn her.

"She is not the only one!" Tess said angrily, and handed Crimshaw her bonnet.

Chapter Four

When Tess stopped to tidy her hair at the mirror before entering the saloon, she was confronted by the familiar expression of Saint Jerome. She adjusted her frown to a smile, for her new role of flirt. This incident must be handled carefully. She would not say Lord James had kidnapped her; that might very well incite Mama to competition for the eel. Lord James was not the issue; Revel would handle *him*. The idea Tess hoped to convey was that she had lost track of time while out with a fairly amusing gentleman. Surely that would nudge Mama into a fit of propriety.

"Mama, you'll never guess what!" Tess said, entering the saloon with a smile. "I met your beau at Lady Revel's, and we went for a drive."

"Lord James!" Mrs. Marchant exclaimed. She was completely floored at this unexpected piece of news, and hardly knew what tack to take. "What the devil did he want with you? Where were you till such an hour? It is long past teatime."

"We were here, there, and everywhere. We drove to Sydney Gardens and had tea at a little shop there. I had no idea he was so amusing."

"I hope you did not think I have been stepping out with a flat. Of course he is amusing."

"Amusing, but somewhat tiresome," Tess said, stifling an imaginary yawn.

"What did he say about me?"

"We did not discuss you much," Tess said, as if to try to remember a single speech. "He thinks I look like the Duchess of Devonshire."

"Idiot! You look nothing whatsoever like the late duchess. *I* am the one who resembles Georgiana. Everyone says so. James himself has mentioned the likeness a dozen times. He was merely buttering you up to get on my good side."

Tess gave a bored look and said, "Very likely. I noticed the lack of invention in his compliments."

"You must have given him a fine opinion of your manners, missing tea without even letting your mother know. That is no way for a young lady to behave."

"I daresay he knows you are not so particular as other mothers in where Dulcie and I go, and what we do."

"I should think I could trust a lady your age to keep an eye on Dulcie!" she flashed back. "I was married with two children by the time I was your age. How did James come to be in our carriage? He has his own."

"He lost a wheel in a race yesterday."

"Nothing of the sort. It had four wheels last night."

Tess did not have to feign surprise at this, but laughter was difficult to simulate. "The sly rascal. He just said so to get into my carriage."

Tess's behavior was so different from what Mrs. Marchant expected that she hardly knew what to say. "Don't take it as a compliment to yourself, miss. He only did it to please me."

"So you said, Mama. You must remember to thank him, if you happen to see him again."

"I shall be seeing him this very evening. He is taking me to a card parlor he knows of, a private club."

"A gaming hall, you mean?" Tess demanded in very much her old way.

"A private club," Mrs. Marchant repeated.

"Perhaps you will meet Papa and Esmée there," Dulcie said.

"Perhaps we shall." Mrs. Marchant smiled.

Dulcie said, "You have not mentioned our new hairstyles, Tess. Are they not charming?"

"Very nice," Tess said, with an air of indifference. The coiffures were in the latest jet, more flattering to Dulcie than her mother. Perhaps she would have her own hair styled. Goading Mama into propriety would require a few beaux, which meant greater attention to her toilette.

Tess went to her room to scheme, and to prepare for the evening. Envisaging an outing to the Lower Rooms, she dressed with care in a russet silk gown with green ribbons. She confided her secret meeting with Lady Revel to Dulcie. "I believe Lord James is only coming tonight to make his apologies to Mama and leave," she explained. "He will not continue courting her. Lord Revel promised to take care of it, so perhaps Mama will take us to the assembly."

"You found Lord Revel obliging then?" Dulcie asked.

"Actually it was Lady Revel who spoke to him."

"Why are you blushing, Tess?" Dulcie asked, grinning.

"I am not blushing."

33

"He's very handsome."

"Yes, he is good-looking. It is the eyes especially—" Tess drew herself back to attention. "Of course the man is a rake."

"Yes, that is certainly part of his charm," Dulcie said. "Do you think Mama will take us to the Assembly Rooms?"

"She hates to stay at home. There will be some vulgar gossip, but her appearing without Papa will not look so bad when she is not with Lord James. Many ladies chaperone their daughters without their husbands tagging along."

"I am glad I had my hair done," Dulcie said, and ran along to her room to prepare her toilette. When Mrs. Marchant was going out, Henshaw had no time to spare for youngsters.

The ladies deceitfully wished their mama a pleasant evening when she took her leave of them after dinner, then waited in expectation of her stormy return. They were sorely disappointed. When they rushed belowstairs at the sound of the closing door, they were told by Crimshaw that the mistress had gone out.

"With Lord James?" Tess demanded.

"Yes, Miss Marchant. She told me not to wait up for her—she had her key—but I am to leave a light burning downstairs."

"The deceiver!" Tess exclaimed, and strode into the saloon.

Dulcie was in a fit of the sulks. She asked Crimshaw to send a pot of cocoa to her room. "I shall be in bed, reading the *Castle of Otranto*," she announced dolefully, as if she were going to the stake.

Tess poured herself a glass of sherry and stared at the Bath stove, where a weak blaze flickered desultorily. What had gone wrong? **Lord Revel** was supposed to have showed his uncle the error of his ways. Mama should have been feeling guilty by now, but no. She had told Crimshaw not to wait up for her, which meant she would be out till all hours. Obviously stronger medicine was called for. For half an hour Tess remained in the saloon, alternately sitting and pacing, trying to invent a new plan.

When the door knocker sounded she stopped pacing and listened to hear who had come to call. Papa! was always the first caller who flew into all their heads when the knocker sounded. She listened, half frightened. That arrogant voice was not Papa's. It sounded like Lord Revel. Impossible!

"Lord Revel," Crimshaw announced.

Hard on his heels came Revel himself, elegantly attired in black evening clothes of exquisite cut, smiling politely and saying he hoped he was not interrupting her. His blue eyes examined her with some interest.

That russet gown set off her ivory skin and ebony hair. Her hairstyle was simple, enlivened with a pearl clasp. The gown was cut rather plainly, but the severe lines showed off her figure. Tess had the best figure of all the Marchants, in his opinion. His preference was for tall ladies. He knew a saint when he saw one, however, and had not come to flirt. In fact, he was somewhat in awe of Tess. As flirtation was his normal mode of behavior with any lady younger than forty, he hardly knew how to behave.

"What is there to interrupt?" Tess replied, with a rebukeful stare. "Mama is out again—with your uncle. They are going to a gaming hall, if you please."

35

"Shall we sit down?" he suggested, as Tess had not taken a seat.

"What do you want?" she asked bluntly. "You must have some reason for calling. I hope Lady Revel is not unwell?"

He remained standing. "She is fine, barring her sore toes. I came to report on my conversation with James. And also to enquire how you enjoyed the Sydney Gardens," he added, with a tentative smile.

"How the devil did you know about that!"

"I thought it a wise precaution to follow you when James invented that plumper about a broken wheel. Figgs told me he had driven his own carriage."

"Then Mama was right," she said frowning, and thoughtlessly sat on the edge of the sofa. Revel took it for permission to be seated and occupied a chair. "She said his carriage was not broken last night. Why on earth would he lie about it?"

"Because he wanted an excuse into your carriage. Perhaps he hopes to transfer his affections from mother to daughter," he suggested. Brave James, he added to himself.

A laugh of disbelief escaped Tess's lips. "Don't be absurd! Mama is much prettier. Besides, Lord James is as old as the hills."

"But not so green. When I disabused him of the notion that your mama owned Northbay outright, he enquired how the daughters were fixed. Like a fool, I told him your dowry."

"And you think he has designs on it? You cannot be serious. Oh, no, you are surely mistaken, or why is he out with Mama again?"

"The date was made earlier; he would not wish to antagonize her by breaking it. They may have

36

one or two other outings lined up, but I have his word he will not make any more assignations."

"That is very kind of you, Lord Revel, but I fear your uncle is not the real problem. I have been giving this considerable thought, and I fear Mama will only latch on to some other hedgebird if Lord James shabs off on her." Revel swallowed that "hedgebird" without blinking, although he was surprised at the lady's plainspeaking. "Are you saying, then, that Lord James's pockets are entirely to let? That it is only Mama's fortune he is after?"

"I did not say 'only.' Your mama is still a lovely lady."

"But you also implied he was after *my* dot."

"Then by induction, you may assume you, too, are a lovely lady. That is a compliment, Miss Marchant."

"Yes, to my dowry, I think."

"I shall try to do better next time. Perhaps a glass of wine would sharpen my wits."

"Oh, certainly. I assumed you would be in a hurry to dash off to some do or other." She poured him a glass of sherry and refilled her own.

"I can drink this up quickly, if you are going out," he said, wondering at her elegant toilette.

"I am not going anywhere. I wasted my time getting all dressed up in the vain hope that Lord James would call off and Mama would take Dulcie and me to the Lower Rooms."

Lord Revel's wish was for a quick escape. "Surely you can chaperone Dulcie," he said, without thinking. Her angry glare told him he had been tactless.

"I have not set up as a chaperone yet, milord!"

To apologize would be to admit his error. He tried to turn it into a compliment. "Your dignity led me

37

astray. You have such a serious manner, one does not think of you in terms of—" Oh, dear, this was rapidly careening toward disaster. "All your church work, and so on," he said vaguely.

"You have made your point, Lord Revel, but I fear the quizzes of Bath would not share your views."

In the end, it was a combination of Tess's improved toilette and his own embarrassment that led him into folly. "I'll take you to the assembly, if you wish. I am on my way there now." As soon as the offer was out, he regretted his lapse of wisdom. He expected a joyous outcry, gratitude, even a note of disbelief at her good fortune, followed by a long evening of boredom.

Tess considered his offer a moment in dull silence, then said, "Dulcie has already gone to bed, and truth to tell, I have a nagging headache. It is the sherry. I had a rather big glass before you came."

His surprise soon rose to annoyance at her refusal. "I expect you have some headache powders in the house."

"Yes, but . . ." She examined Lord Revel. The most handsome, eligible gentleman in town had just asked her out, so why was she declining? On those few occasions when she stood up with him at the local assemblies, the dance was pure torture. She never knew what to say to him. Half the time she didn't even know what he was talking about. His conversation was affected and cynical. To spend a whole evening in his company seemed too much of a strain, particularly in her present troubled state.

He waited. "Yes, but—?"

"I did want to make Mama think I was carrying on with some gentleman, so she would worry about me, and hopefully begin to think about propriety. She has no more notion of propriety than a cat, Lord Revel. It is really quite shocking. I daresay if I were out with you, however, even Mama might worry."

Revel just blinked in astonishment. When he found his tongue, he said in blighting accents, "She would have to be lax indeed to let *that* pass without sending for the constable!"

Tess looked aghast at what she had said. Her fingers flew to her lips in consternation. "Oh, dear. I did not mean— It is just that she knows your reputation."

"So I gathered."

"I'm sure you are not as bad as everyone says," she said, hoping to lessen her offense.

"Then why do you hesitate to come with me?" he asked.

"You don't quite understand what I am saying."

"I think I do, but if I misunderstand, then you are saying your piece badly, Miss Marchant. Marshal your thoughts, and tell me what the problem is." Anger was deteriorating to curiosity, and even amusement at her predicament.

"Well, it is all rather complicated. I am trying to reform Mama. Just going to an assembly is not enough. I need some biddable fellow who will meet me for secret trysts in gardens, and keep me out late, and generally make Mama think I am being indiscreet, so that she will worry and nag. She cannot rag at me if she is playing the hoyden herself, so she will have to pull in her own horns."

"I can be the very soul of indiscretion," he said, warming to the novel idea. Revel was finding Bath dull since he had dropped his latest flirt. This was a caper much to his taste. It would enliven the few weeks of his mama's visit. Tess was by no means an antidote. It might be amusing to have a harmless flirtation with a lady so different from his usual friends. Best of all, they both knew it was in jest.

"I know it," she said, "but that is not what I want. I want someone harmless, who will not be trying to kiss me . . . or anything like that. I have no intention of really *being* a loose woman you must know, Lord Revel. I just want Mama to think so."

"Short of hiring an actor, Miss Marchant, I doubt you will find what you want, even in staid old Bath. You could find many a gent who would not give you a moment's worry about kissing you behind bushes. Your greatest fear would be dying of boredom, but then such a man would not worry your mama much, either, would he? No sane gent would put his reputation at risk, and the insane sort could not be counted on to be so biddable as you require."

"You're right. It was an idiotic idea."

"Why do you keep avoiding the obvious?"

"Hiring an actor, you mean? I wouldn't know how—"

He drew a weary sigh. "No, ma'am. I was referring to Lord Revel." He performed a graceful bow. "You have before you a man vastly experienced in trifling with a lady's affections. I have no reputation to lose, and I will solemnly undertake not to kiss you behind any bushes. You and I understand that you will not take advantage of the situation to bullox me into an offer of marriage." He pierced her with a gleam from his flashing blue eyes.

"I have not the least wish to marry you!"

"The feeling is mutual. I will not push discretion to the point where you are publicly branded as a harlot. Our indiscretions will be for your mama's eyes only."

She listened closely, and when he fell silent, she

spoke. "Why would you bother? It will be a dull scald for you, having to jaunter about town with me."

"You underestimate yourself, Miss Marchant. Besides," he added more truthfully, "Mama's annual visits to Bath are always a dull scald for me."

"Then I am surprised you come with her."

"Contrary to popular report, I am not composed one hundred percent of selfishness. The visits have become a tradition. In the winter we come to Bath for a month for our health. Mama drinks the waters and I vegetate. She tells me it is the only time of the year she sees me for more than two days running. For some unaccountable reason she likes to see her son on a daily basis from time to time. I rather enjoy seeing her, too, as a matter of fact."

Tess listened, and after a pause, she took her decision. "If you're sure you have nothing better to do, then I accept, Lord Revel. It is very kind of you. I never thought you would be the sort to—" He lowered his brows in a mock-menacing way. "I shall tell Dulcie I'm leaving now."

"Perhaps she would like to come with us?"

"Oh, no! We don't want her along. How can we misbehave with a youngster to look after? We may have to stay out pretty late if I am to come home after Mama. That is the sort of thing I had in mind, to make her worry, you know. Are you sure you want to go on with this, Lord Revel?"

"Quite sure."

"Then it will be better if we just sneak out without telling Dulcie. I'll have Crimshaw send a servant up for my pelisse."

"And the headache powders. I can tell you from experience, it is impossible to carry on a successful dalliance with a lady who has the megrims."

She touched her fingers to her temples. "My headache seems to be gone. Perhaps it was just frustration." A warm and natural smile beamed at him. "I never imagined it would be so exciting, misbehaving like this."

Revel rose and offered her his hand. "See what you have been missing all these years, Miss Marchant?" he said in an insinuating voice.

Their eyes met and held a moment. It looked very like a challenge in Revel's gaze. Fear tinged with pleasure gazed back at him.

Tess called Crimshaw and told him she was going out with Lord Revel. He need not inform Miss Dulcie unless she asked.

"By then it will be too late for her to do anything about it," she explained to Lord Revel.

Crimshaw returned with the pelisse, and Lord Revel placed it over Tess's shoulders. He stood behind her. His head leaned forward and he said softly in her ear, "All set for a night of wild debauchery, Tess?"

A shiver scuttled up her spine at the sound of his voice reverberating in her ear. She cast a frightened peep over her shoulder. "You called me Tess. You never did that before."

"I always call my flirts by their first names. You may call me Revel."

When Revel placed her hand on his arm and led her out, Crimshaw looked stiff with disapproval. Tess feared she had chosen her flirt unwisely. She also felt a giddy tingle of excitement to be misbehaving for the first time in her life.

Chapter Five

The Lower Rooms were bulging with company by the time Lord Revel and Tess arrived at the assembly. Heads turned to ogle Revel's new flirt. As Tess had made so few forays into society, she was not recognized by many, but the few who knew her were busy to spread all the scandal.

"Her mama is no better than she should be. No doubt the daughter is the same."

"That would suit young Lord Revel right down to the heels."

"Nonsense, a man does not dirty his own backyard. The Marchants are close neighbors of the Revels in the country. And the girl has a good dowry."

"A match, then?"

Tess's fingers clutched at Revel's arm as at a lifeline. "Everyone is whispering!" she said in a low voice.

"Excellent! Word is bound to get back to your mama. A pity they don't play any waltzes at these dos. There is something so very respectable about the cotillion. But I promise to do my poor best to raise eyebrows, Tess."

"You will not have to try. I see you raise eyebrows by just entering a room."

They joined a square, and for the length of the dance, Revel flirted admirably. Languishing glances and soft smiles were bestowed on Tess when the steps of the dance took them apart, and when they were together, he spoke softly, to give the idea their conversation was too intimate for other ears.

"Evans is planning to ask you for the next set," he whispered.

"How do you know?"

"By the calculating way he is looking at you. I shall play the jealous lover and carry you off for tea."

"Good! I should love a cup of tea. I ought to have taken that headache powder after all. My temples are pinching again. I feel like a filly up at auction, with everyone staring at me. I don't know how you can stand it, Revel."

"And here you thought my life was a bed of roses."

"Liberally sprinkled with thorns," she added. "I am not so foolish as to imagine a high flyer has an easeful life."

"You'll get used to the altitude. When I made my maiden speech in the House, I received some excellent advice from the Duke of Devonshire. Pretend all the people staring at you are stark naked, and they will soon lose their power to intimidate. I still practice the trick from time to time."

"On the ladies, I wager!" she scolded.

"You read me like a book, Tess."

As he had prophecied, Evans appeared beside them at the cotillion's end. "Miss Marchant, may I have the honor?"

Revel put a possessive arm around Tess's waist

and said, "Miss Marchant is not feeling very well, Evans. We are going to take tea."

Evans said what was expected. "I am very sorry to hear it, Miss Marchant. Perhaps later?"

"Perhaps," Revel said jealously, and led her off to the tearoom, where he avoided all the company beckoning to him and chose a table for two.

"There were two very handsome bachelors at that table, Revel," she pointed out.

"You have already chosen your rake, madam. We are like horses; dangerous to change in midstream."

"A pity all the handsome men are rakes." She sighed. It was possible to infer a compliment in this complaint, and he let it pass. "I should like to have a dance with Evans later," she said. "I have been casting sheep's eyes at him all week on Milsom Street, and he never spared me a glance. It is my being with you that has raised me in his esteem."

"Watch your words, Tess. You are skating dangerously close to a compliment there."

She made a little moue and laughed. Revel was intrigued with the change in her. Excitement lent a sparkle to her eyes and a flush to her cheeks. Nothing, however, altered the blunt nature of her speech. "I only meant he probably thinks I am fast. He has a little reputation with the ladies."

"Odd you were casting sheep's eyes at such a rattle."

"I am not at all so nice in my demands as you seem to think, Revel. At my advanced age, you know, and with the scandal hovering over the family, I must grab whatever sort of *parti* I can get my hands on. At least he is not a fortune hunter. Mama says he has a dandy estate in Kent."

"I see Mama is not entirely derelict in her guardianship."

"She can see a fortune hunter by daylight."

"It is by moonlight they must be watched," he warned.

After tea, Tess had her dance with Evans. She found him a dead bore after Revel's company, but forged on with the acquaintance. He was given permission to call at Bartlett Street the next day. Other gentlemen stood up with her, and before leaving, she had a second dance with Revel.

"This will set the old cats to meowing," she said, laughing. "A second dance is a forerunner to an engagement in Bath. Mama is bound to hear of this."

"We'll give her more than this to worry about. Let us go for a drive after, and return at one o'clock."

"Or later, if she is not home yet," Tess said.

"How will we know? I foresee a long wait, huddling in shadows for her to return, only to learn she has been home all along."

"No, she'll turn out the lights when she goes to bed."

The assembly was over at eleven. They drove straight to Bartlett Street, to see if the lights were still burning. They were, which left them with the problem of where to go for the next hour or two.

"A pity the circulating library is closed," Tess said. "I can spend hours poring over the books."

"A great pity," Revel agreed, chewing a grin. "We shall drive into the Crescent Gardens and see whose carriage is where it shouldn't be."

"What do you mean, Revel?"

As this revealed his own scarlet past, he ignored

the question. "Or we could just take a spin into the countryside."

"I don't understand. Why would anyone go to the Crescent Gardens so late at night? They could not see the flowers."

"They could smell them."

"They go there to *cuddle*!" she exclaimed. "That is what you meant!"

" 'Cuddle' is one word for it, I suppose."

"I'm surprised your team did not head in that direction from habit."

"There is more than one place to take a wayward lady. I prefer a discreet inn in the country," he said airily.

"I prefer the Crescent Gardens. Let us go there at once."

He snapped to attention. *"What?"*

"To see if Lord James's carriage is there, stoopid! I hope you didn't think I planned to let you have your way with me."

"I don't want to have my way with you! This is fine gratitude for all my efforts to help you."

"I have been wondering about that. I cannot quite trust disinterested help from you, for your mama always says you are the most selfish beast in nature."

"What possible good can I hope to gain from helping you?" he demanded hotly.

"I think you want to get Esmée back by making her jealous, since Papa stole her from you, and it amuses you to use me to do it."

"Who says I want her back?"

"I haven't heard you have taken up with anyone else."

"Perhaps my amorous career is on hiatus."

"Hiatus? What is that?"

"Pardon me. The word has three syllables," he said through thin lips.

"How very rude you are! I know lots of words with three syllables."

"Of course you do. There is cowcumber, and nip-farthing."

"Don't forget reprobate!" she added, with a bold smile.

"Add ingratitude to your list, milady."

"That is four syllables. I count, too, you see. Oh, look, Revel!" She grabbed his arm. "That is Lord James's carriage, is it not? And it's only eleven-thirty. He is bringing her home pretty early. We'll wait till Mama goes in. I want her to have a few minutes to worry about me. Say half an hour. We shall just park here in the shadows."

"I cannot leave my nags standing in this cold for half an hour!"

"Why do gentlemen invariably put the welfare of their cattle before that of ladies?" she snipped.

Undeterred, Revel pulled the check string and directed John Groom to trot the nags along the Upper Bristol Road a few miles, then return, but they waited to see Lord James escort Mrs. Marchant to her front door.

"We should have waited to see if she invited him inside," Tess complained as the carriage rolled away.

"We'll see if his rig is still there when we return."

"What, leave his nags standing in the cold for half an hour? Impossible!"

"I should think you would be a little more conciliating, Tess. I am going a mile out of my way to help you."

"I do hope it brings Esmée round your thumb, Revel. Fancy her preferring Papa to you. Some ladies do like a little maturity in their flirts, of course."

"Are you implying I am immature?"

"A gentleman of one and thirty who has had a series of mistresses, but is afraid to settle down, must be considered immature," she pointed out blandly. "I feel Esmée must agree with me."

"I turned Esmée off two weeks ago."

"Why? What is wrong with her? I must warn Papa. Is she very expensive?"

"On the contrary. She refused to take anything. Money, jewelry . . ."

"Surely that is all to the good," she said in confusion.

"No, it is not all to the good. When a lady refuses payment, it means she expects something else for her trouble. To wit, a wedding ring."

"Oh, dear! Poor Papa! I must warn him."

Revel was annoyed with Tess. He felt he was doing her a tremendous favor, and all he was getting for his trouble was complaints and insults. Eventually he would no doubt star as the wrongdoer in the affair when she was kind enough to jilt him. He must be mad. He was beginning to have serious doubts about this undertaking. He might shift the job off on to Evans. Yet that did not quite please him, either.

The lights were still burning at Bartlett Street when the carriage returned. Lord James's carriage was nowhere in sight.

"He has either left, or he is having his groom drive the nags around," Revel said.

"Since the window curtains are open, we can peek in the saloon window and see if he is there," Tess suggested. "I shall also be interested to see if they are kissing."

"I refuse to play the Peeping Tom!"

"Don't be so missish, Revel."

"Missish" was the last charge Revel ever expected to hear hurled at his head. He had been castigated before for flying too high, driving too fast, gambling too deep, and other conduct becoming a bachelor about town, but "missish"! This was really the outside of enough.

Tess was already opening her door and dismounting. Revel climbed out the other door and followed her toward the house. The window was rather high. Even on tiptoe, Revel could not see in, and Tess's head was six inches below the frame.

"I'll have to lift you up," he said.

"You'd never get me off the ground. I weigh nine stone."

Annoyed at yet another slur on his manhood, Revel put his hands around her waist and lifted her off the ground. She grabbed on to the window ledge and peered through the curtains. Vision was misty through the layers of chiffon, but she could see her mama, bathed in light from the lamp. She was idly flipping through a magazine. "Lord James is not there," she said, and Revel let her slide to the ground.

Her body brushed intimately against his as he lowered her. She was acutely aware of his arms pressing her waist, and the shadowed eyes regarding her. With both feet on the ground, she looked up and said in a breathless voice, "I am down now. You can let me go, Revel. I'll go right in now."

"Not without my mark on you," he said softly, and tightened his hold until she was crushed against his chest.

She mistrusted that glitter in his eyes. "What do you mean?" she demanded, frowning at him.

"I mean—this," he said. His head descended, his lips touched hers and clung. Caught by surprise, Tess let him get away with it. It was a new experience for her to be kissed by such a dasher and she savored it objectively. It was rather nice. There was some excitement in feeling a man so close, with his skin actually pressing on hers, but she felt none of that swooning that her friends spoke of. Neither did she feel the least frightened. It was not until Revel's lips firmed and the pressure increased that the giddiness invaded her head. She put both hands on his chest and pushed him away.

"You promised you wouldn't!" she accused.

"Now who is being missish?" he taunted.

"I take leave to tell you, Revel, I *am* a miss. There is nothing wrong in *my* being missish."

"I only promised not to kiss you behind bushes, Tess." He laughed. "Your mama is no flat. She can tell the difference between a lady who has been arguing like a shrew and one who has been cuddling." He noticed, however, that Tess still resembled the former.

"Do I look wanton?" she asked.

"Like a debauched seraphim."

"Angels have blond hair, Revel. Everyone knows that."

"I stand corrected," he said, with unsteady lips. "I should have said a debauched schoolmarm."

They began walking to the front door. "It is odd you should say that. I have often wanted to be a schoolmarm."

"And not an actress? Your imagination is sadly deficient, Tess."

"The hurly-burly of the chaise longue has no allure for me."

"I never denigrate a thing until I have tried it," he said mischievously.

They reached the door and stopped. Revel lifted his fingers and rubbed them hard on her lips. "As you object to reality, we'll create the illusion of riotous flirtation by other means. Now go, while your lips are still red."

Tess ran her hands through her coiffure to tousle it while Revel watched, bemused. Odd how those few touches of the wanton improved Tess's appearance. They removed her air of awful propriety.

"She'll never believe I was with you. She will think it was some flat," she said.

"I'll go in and make our mutual apologies."

"She can be very snarky when she is in one of her moods. Let me handle her."

"I shall call on you tomorrow to verify your story then."

"Mr. Evans is coming tomorrow, but you come, too. It will increase his interest if he sees such a swell as you in the saloon."

Revel just shook his head in confusion. These artless speeches told him that in some impersonal way, Tess realized he was a prime *parti*, but it didn't impress her. She was just using him, and she took every care to let him know it. It was a sad comedown for him. He reached the doorknob, twisted it, and said, "The door's locked. Do you have a key with you?"

"No, I never take a key. I don't have one." He lightly tapped the knocker. "Run along now, Revel."

His gentlemanly instincts rebelled at this, or perhaps it was at her dismissive "Run along." He was still there when the door opened and Mrs. Marchant glared out.

Chapter Six

"I hope you have a very good excuse for coming home at such an hour—" Mrs. Marchant's glaring eyes espied Lord Revel and she stopped in mid-speech.

He immediately stepped forward, wearing a smile that had been charming ladies into forgiveness for a decade. "Mrs. Marchant, pray do not scold Tess. The fault is entirely mine."

The dame's angry scowl softened to girlish delight. "Lord Revel! Do come in for a glass of wine. My manners are gone begging. I'm sure there is some perfectly innocent explanation for this."

They were ushered into the saloon. "Revel called and took me to the Lower Rooms," Tess explained.

"So Crimshaw told me, dear, but the Lower Rooms close at eleven o'clock," she said, casting a steely glance at her daughter. "It has just rung twelve."

"The evening was so fine we felt like a spin. I do hope you were not too worried, Mrs. Marchant," Revel said in a drawling voice, as though a midnight spin in winter were a common occurence.

"Of course, but where did you go at such an hour?"

"A few miles out past the Lower Commons. We hardly left town," he assured her. Any other mother would have combed his hair with a footstool. He began to appreciate the size of the job he had undertaken in trying to bring this hussy to a sense of her duties.

"Get Revel a glass of wine, Tess. Where are your manners?"

Tess poured three glasses of wine and passed them. Mrs. Marchant's mind was not deep, but it was quick. She soon latched on to the idea that Tess had caught Revel's interest. It took her a moment to assimilate such an unlikely thing, but what else could it mean? Lady Revel or someone had told Revel it was time to settle down. He had chosen a wife who would be content to stay at Revel Hall while he trotted off to London and Brighton, and had settled on Tess. Mrs. Marchant could hardly believe her daughter's great fortune.

She looked to Tess in wonderment. It was then that she noticed Tess's mussed hair, and the unaccustomed rosiness of her lips. If she didn't know better, she would think the girl had been kissing. Surely it *was* marriage Revel had in mind? If it was not, he would soon learn a gentleman did not dally with a Marchant without paying the price.

It was her role as chaperone to let him know Tess was not a plaything. "I was worried," she confided to Revel, with that air of the lady who is accustomed to admiration. "Tess is such an innocent babe! She would let herself be imposed on by a gentleman. Since it is you, dear Revel, naturally I forgive you *this time*," she said playfully. "One knows your attentions are honorable."

He read the lady's mind to a T. "I promise you Tess was in no way compromised. I regret if I caused you a moment's fear."

"In future, it will be best if you can bring Tess straight home from any little outing. You cannot imagine my palpitations when I came home and found her gone. I have been sitting here for hours, worrying my fingers to the bone."

Tess and Revel exchanged a laughing look at this blatant lie. "You are too kind, Mrs. Marchant. I shall bear your wishes in mind, if Tess and I ever go out again."

Tess bit back a small smile. Revel was performing marvelously. He knew her wish to worry Mama, and was not putting himself forward as a serious suitor. He finished his wine, rose, and took his leave.

Mrs. Marchant's smiles left with him. It was an angry, calculating face that turned to confront Tess. "Widgeon!" she exclaimed angrily. "I had some hope the family had ordered him to settle down, but it is no such thing. He is merely bored to flinders, and has settled on you to pass the time. You'll never get *that* one to the altar, miss, so don't cast your reputation to the wind for his sake."

"We only went for a little drive, Mama."

"It is twelve o'clock, Tess."

"But you said twelve o'clock is early."

"It is not early for a young girl. I find it exceedingly odd a little drive should put such a color in your lips. I was not born yesterday, Tess. I am shocked at your behavior. If Revel were serious, he would have taken Dulcie to the Lower Rooms with you. You should have thought of that yourself. I am surprised he hit on you, for in the usual way, he never tampers with girls from good families."

"I wonder if he thinks our family is not quite the

thing, now that you and Papa are getting divorced," Tess suggested slyly.

"What has that to do with anything?"

"You said Dulcie cannot be presented if you are divorced, so obviously it *does* make a difference, Mama."

Mrs. Marchant flinched at this touch of the serpent's tooth. She was worldly enough to realize the danger to her daughters in the pending divorce. "In any case, I let Revel know he is not to carry on in this way in future. If he comes sniffing around again, we will assume he is serious. I mean that he plans to marry you," she added, to make her meaning perfectly clear. "And if he does not, then you must not see him."

"How was your evening, Mama?" Tess asked. She hoped to hear that Lord James had given her her congé.

"Wretched. I lost two guineas, and the supper they served was inedible. Cold meat and bread. I told James I would not care to visit the place with him again. We are going to a play tomorrow night."

Tess wished to discover whether this was one of the appointments that had been made before Revel spoke to his cousin. "I think you mentioned the play before?" she said.

"Very likely. James has subscription tickets, so he feels he must go to get his money's worth. I would much rather go to a rout."

This did not quite answer Tess's question. "Where else do you and James plan to go?" she asked.

"Good gracious, it is a romance, not a military campaign. We don't have the whole season planned in advance." Not a word was said about breaking the affair off. Her next speech was, "I don't suppose you saw your papa at the assembly?"

"No, he could not take Esmée there."

"I should hope not, but she is so brazen she would go to Court with a married man. If Bath takes us for fallen women, Tess, you must not blame me. It is all in your father's dish."

"Society has always granted men more freedom in that respect. It is only when a lady carries on that the family's reputation sinks."

"Don't talk nonsense, child. There is scarcely a married lady in London who goes anywhere with her husband. It is very poor ton to do so. The mischief in our situation is that your papa left home. If he at least resided under the same roof, nothing would be thought of it."

"You are the one who put him out, Mama."

"This time he went too far," Mrs. Marchant said grimly, but there were tears glittering in her eyes, and more grief than anger on her pinched face. "He ought not to have done it in Bath."

"Bath is more strict than most cities," Tess agreed.

"Strict? What do I care for strict? It was in Bath that he met and courted me, Tess. We were married at home and came back here for our honeymoon. Lyle never carried on with lightskirts in Bath before. It is like flirting in church. I could not forgive that. I am only kept in my skin by the hope that he will come back and beg my forgiveness."

Her control flew to the winds, and she dissolved in a bout of tears. Tess felt sorry for her mother, and guilty for adding to her troubles. Mama couldn't help being a peagoose. She had put up with a good deal from her husband. If Mama loved him less, this never would have happened. She would have turned her head the other way and gone on pretending not to know, or to mind. It was the fate of ladies who married men like Papa, or Lord Revel.

Both ladies took their confusion and troubles to bed with them. Mrs. Marchant now had to worry that her little fling with James was jeopardizing her daughters' reputations. She was bored to flinders with James. Her jaws ached from trying to swallow her yawns after an evening with him. They only went to hole-in-the-wall places, which was her fault. If James were seeing an unattached lady, they would be welcome anywhere. She worried about Tess and Revel. There was no trusting a fellow like Revel, though it would be wonderful if Tess could nab him. Certainly the pair of them had been kissing, which was shocking. Tess should have more sense, but then who could resist a dashing fellow like Revel?

There was more to Tess than she had realized. James, too, had spoken warmly of her. A little more warmly than Mrs. Marchant quite liked. "A charming girl," he had said so often she wanted to crown him.

Perhaps men saw something in Tess that evaded her own feminine eyes? It was not only beauty that attracted men, but some other intangible aura of sexuality. Personally she had never glimpsed such a thing in Tess. If Tess nabbed Revel, she would be a countess! With such powerful connections, what was to stop Dulcie from becoming a duchess?

Tess's thoughts, while different, were equally troublesome. Until that night, she had not realized how much Mama still loved Papa. It seemed hard to add to her worries at this troubled time, yet something must be done. Papa would not come home while Lord James was in the picture.

Breakfast was an unpleasant affair, with Dulcie in the boughs at Tess's trick of darting off to the Lower Rooms without her. A little ray of light penetrated the gloom when Tess mentioned that Mr. Evans was to call that afternoon.

"The man you used to ogle at the Pump Room?" Dulcie asked. "The one with the long nose?"

"His nose is not long!"

"Why did you not tell me Evans is calling?" Mrs. Marchant demanded. "This is wonderful news. He has five thousand a year if he has a sou. And he cannot be too high in the instep, for his mama married a dancing master when his papa died. It was a great secret; everyone was whispering it."

Dulcie burst into peals of laughter. "I don't think he ought to be encouraged," she said.

"Beggars cannot be choosers," the mama retorted. "With your father making a scandal of us, we are fortunate for friendship from any half-decent source. And Evans is half decent. His papa was a gentleman, even if his mama is a goosecap."

As the ladies would be remaining at home in the afternoon, they took the carriage out for a spin in the morning. The main point of interest in these drives was to scour the streets for a sight of Mr. Marchant and/or Mrs. Gardener, and if they spotted the latter, to see what she was wearing. She was glimpsed coming out of the milliner's, but she was not with her new beau. The carriage was immediately stopped and the three ladies descended to follow Mrs. Gardener for a block, at which point she got into her own carriage and disappeared, without realizing she had been under observation.

Chapter Seven

Mrs. Marchant made the supreme sacrifice of lending Henshaw to the girls for their toilettes that afternoon. Fearful for Tess's burgeoning powers of attractions, she said, "If young Evans suggests a ride, Tess, you will take Dulcie with you."

"I cannot leave," Tess said. "Someone else might call."

Her mother gave her a look, half-pitying, half-disdainful. "If you refer to Revel, I would not sit home waiting for him to come. He made it pretty clear last night. '*If* Tess and I ever go out again,' he said, bold as brass. And calling you Tess, too. He never did that before, now I think of it."

"I was not necessarily referring to Revel. I met other gentlemen as well last night."

Mrs. Marchant, watching Tess's reflection in the mirror, decided it was the mirror that gave Tess that sly expression, like a cat. Yet the girl had certainly changed her stripes in the space of twenty-four hours. That very morning Mrs. Marchant had been required to answer the letters from Northbay, for Tess had not done it as she usually did. A grudging admiration was sneaking in with the annoyance.

When the young ladies were as pretty as Henshaw's clever hands could make them, they went belowstairs to await Evans's arrival. He came punctually at three, bearing a bunch of indifferent posies picked up from a street vendor. No sooner had he made his bows than his long nose and eager eye turned to Dulcie, sitting in all the glory of her new *cheribime* do, with the sun striking her blond curls, turning them to gold.

"I don't believe I have had the pleasure of your . . . friend's acquaintance," he said to Tess.

"This is my little sister, Miss Dulcie," Tess said.

"Not *that* little, Tess," Mrs. Marchant said playfully.

Here was one man who knew true beauty when he saw it, at least. Evans sat down, tea was served, and the conversation ground along dully. Evans did not believe he had seen Miss Dulcie at the Lower Rooms last night. No indeed, she had not gone. She was reading *The Castle of Otranto* and could not tear herself away from the trials of Isabella.

Evans's chair moved a little closer to her, and for the next ten minutes, the room rang with exclamations of delighted horror regarding the wicked Manfred, and Theodore, who bore such an uncanny resemblance to the portrait of Alfonso.

"I know Theodore is not just a simple peasant," Dulcie exclaimed. Evans opened his lips to corroborate it, and she said, "No, don't tell me, Mr. Evans. I have not finished the book yet. I have only been reading it for two weeks."

Mrs. Marchant was nearly convinced her elder daughter was the flat she always knew her to be, for she sat with her tongue between her teeth while Dulcie waltzed away with her beau. The rattle of the door knocker was heard, and suddenly Tess's face became animated.

"Who could that be?' she asked, but she wore a gloating smile. "Why, it is Lord Revel," she exclaimed in poorly simulated surprise when his voice was heard in the hallway. "I wonder what he wants."

When Revel entered and saw Mr. Evans in the room, the smile on his face froze. Revel spoke first to the ladies, but when he addressed Evans, his displeasure was obvious. Indeed in Tess's opinion, it was a tad overdone. He need not have glared quite so fiercely.

Revel was served wine, and for a few moments the conversation veered from *Otranto* into more general waters. Everyone agreed it was a lovely day. The weather very mild for the time of year.

"Let us take advantage of it and go for a spin," Revel suggested, directing his invitation to Tess.

"I cannot leave, Revel," she said, looking at Evans.

"Don't let me detain you," Evans said promptly. "I was about to leave in any case."

"No, no, you must not rush away," Tess insisted.

"Why don't we all go out for a drive?" Evans suggested, turning his long nose to Dulcie.

Mrs. Marchant found no fault in this. She assumed the four would go in one carriage; two of the four knew she thought so, and said not a word to disillusion her. The group left as a foursome, but when they strolled by twos along the street, looking for their carriages, Evans called over his shoulder, "Your carriage or mine, Revel? Or shall we each take our own?"

"Let us go by twos, like Noah's ark," Revel replied.

Dulcie cast a questioning eye at her older sister, fully expecting Tess to scotch this exciting scheme.

Tess said, "Then we shall take our leave of you now, Mr. Evans. It was nice seeing you again. Take care of Dulcie."

When she was safely ensconced in Revel's chaise, she said, "I made sure you would cry craven and not come this afternoon, after Mama's hints last night."

"Surely a carriage drive in full sunlight is not enough to compromise us."

"As long as we are home before dinner."

"Did she cut up stiff after I left?"

"You did not fool her for a moment. She knows full well you are only amusing yourself with me as Bath is so dull. I am not to see you again unless it is clear your intentions are honorable, sir."

"They are not *dis*honorable, but you must not let her get the idea it is to be a match."

"I am rethinking this whole affair, Revel. Mama has enough worries in her dish." She told him about her mother's outburst the night before. "So if she is a little distracted, one can hardly blame her. She still loves him very much, you see."

"I have always thought love matches ought to be outlawed. Whichever of the loving couple recovers his sanity first, pitches the other into misery." He waited, fully expecting a lively argument on the merits of true love.

"I daresay the first weeks of rapture would be delightful, but until some way is found for both to become sane simultaneously, it is a poor bargain," she agreed.

64

"You would limit the rapture to weeks?" he asked, surprised, but ready to shift ground for conversation's sake.

"Perhaps months," she said reflectively.

"I personally know a man who has been happily married for two years," he said.

"He must have married a saint."

"On the contrary; his wife did."

"Poor lady. How can she be happy with a saint? One feels instinctively sinners would be more amusing." She had a passing memory of Saint Jerome. "Have you seen your cousin today?"

"No, did your mama say anything about him?"

"Nothing that suggested the affair is over. She is attending a play with him this evening."

"It will be the last outing. He mentioned the play yesterday. Romeo Coates is to perform one of his vivisections on Shakespeare."

She looked blank. "What do you mean?"

"Never mind, Tess. It is a joke."

"Oh," she said, but was not interested enough to pursue it. "Mama will be twice as blue when Lord James jilts her, too. I am almost sorry I had you speak to him, except that she really does not care for him in the least, and it would be a pity if she broke his heart."

"It is a case of cream-pot love, Tess. As to bringing our 'affair' to a halt, I think you should reconsider. Your intention was to awaken your mother to her duties. It seems you are having some success. If your parents are not to get together, it is more important than ever that Mrs. Marchant behave with propriety. The daughters of a broken marriage are already under a cloud. Throw in a giddy mama, and the better class of gent will stay away in droves."

"But if Papa continues acting the lecher . . . ?"

He shrugged. "Society does not expect much propriety from men. It is the ladies who are saddled with the burden of behaving themselves. You and Dulcie will take your moral coloring from your mother. In fact, society looks with a peculiarly sympathetic eye on such ladies. Being wronged by men recommends them to the more devout sort. If you frequented London, you would realize Byron's wife is in the process of canonization since she had to throw him out."

"One wonders how she could have the heart for it, he is so handsome and romantic," Tess said in a dreamy way.

Revel was amazed that she admired Byron. He would have thought her taste in men more demanding, and intimated something of the sort. "I daresay it is the feminine folly of wanting to tame a rake that incites you to passion."

"Tame Lord Byron? Surely you jest! Propriety would be the ruination of a man like that. His indiscretions are the most interesting thing about him. I nearly gave up on him when he married Miss Milbankes."

"One wonders why she ever married him, if what she wanted was an archbishop, but there you are. A perfect scientific example of opposites attracting—and the rapture of a love match dissipating within weeks." He glanced from the window as he spoke, then gave a startled jerk.

Tess looked to see what had caught his attention and saw Esmée Gardener. At the same moment, she recognized the lady's partner. "It is Papa!" she squealed. "With that horrid woman. Oh, I am sorry, Revel. I forgot she used to be your friend."

"She is still my friend," he said curtly. "We parted amicably."

"Let us follow them and see where they are going." She pulled the check string and the carriage drew to a stop, but Lord Revel did not budge an inch.

"There are limits to how far I am willing to go in this farce, Tess. I refuse to scuttle along Milsom Street, dogging the steps of an erstwhile mistress."

"Of course, I understand," she said at once. "I'll go alone, if you would please open the door."

"You are not going to follow them alone!" he declared.

"Don't try to order me about!" She wrenched open the door and began to get out. Revel closed it and pulled her roughly back onto the seat.

"Where did I ever get the idea you are a sensible girl! You have no more notion of propriety than your mama. Have I not just been telling you ladies in your position must behave like Caesar's wife? What would the quizzes of Bath say if you were seen tagging along behind your father and his mistress?"

She leaned against the window, hardly listening to him. "There! They are getting into her carriage. We'll follow them in yours. What a lovely tilbury she has, and its being green will make it easy to keep track of amid the other carriages."

Revel had to be content with this half victory. At least it kept the foolish chit off the street. They followed the green tilbury along Milsom Street to Quiet Street, thence south to the Upper Bristol Road.

"Where can they be going? Does Mrs. Gardener live nearby?" Tess asked.

"No, she has an apartment in Bridewell Lane."

"It looks as if they are leaving town," Tess said.

"Straying gents usually take their ladybirds to a quiet inn a little out of town for . . ."

She turned a knowing eye on him. "So you told me earlier."

". . . for tea," he said.

Her cool gray stare went through him and raised a blush. "Mama will want to know which inn they are going to. We shall keep after them."

Revel knew, none better, that Esmée did not insist on going to an inn for tea. She had a healthy regard for her reputation and did not entertain gentlemen in her boudoir at her apartment lest the servants gossip, but she would serve a gentleman tea at home. The direction the green tilbury was traveling suggested a little inn tucked away just outside of Keynsham. There was no point purveying all this sordid business to Tess, however.

"I know which inn they are going to," he said. "We'll turn back now."

"Which inn is it?"

"The George and Dragon. Why do you ask?"

"Because as soon as you take me home, I shall call our carriage and drive there."

"They'll be gone long since."

"They will if they are only having tea," she replied.

Revel's patience broke. "What is to be gained by catching them in a compromising situation? It will only embarrass all three of you."

"It won't embarrass *me*. Perhaps it will bring

Papa to his senses. I shall bring Dulcie with me. Papa is very fond of her."

"What of Dulcie's feelings? What of Mrs. Gardener's?"

"A woman like that doesn't deserve to have feelings. I hope she is well and truly ashamed of herself, to be branded an adulteress in front of the family she is breaking up. Take me home at once, Revel."

"You might at least give a thought to Dulcie."

"She knows perfectly well what is going on. Let her see what men are like. It will be a salutary lesson for her before she is carried off to London."

If Tess insisted on going to the George and Dragon—why hadn't he named a different inn?—he must go with her and try to avoid a confrontation. Marchant and Esmée likely would have tea first, hopefully downstairs. Esmée liked to take her tea in a proper parlor. He would send her a note, tipping her a clue Marchant's daughter was at the inn.

He kept a few carriages behind the tilbury, but close enough to see where it was going. When it slowed down just before the George and Dragon, he knew what Esmée had in mind—and braced himself for what could only be an extremely embarrassing business. Marchant and Esmée had entered the inn by the time Revel's carriage reached it.

"Why don't you just stay comfortable here while I nip inside and discover what they are doing?" he suggested.

Tess didn't bother to reply, but just rose and followed him out. "It isn't a very nice inn," she said, flickering a disdainful glance over the crouching little stone building with Norman doorway. "I thought mistresses were treated more royally."

"Only if they are royal mistresses."

"You're a nobleman. I'm surprised you brought her here, and I am surprised at Papa, too."

"Don't take your ill-humor out on me, miss. This is not my fault."

"I didn't say it was," she retorted, and strode angrily toward the rounded doorway.

The first people they spotted inside were Marchant and Mrs. Gardener. They were at the clerk's desk, just signing the register. Esmée spotted Revel and arranged a triumphant smile. Then she glanced to see what new chick he had picked up, and her handsome eyes started from their sockets. She did not officially have the acquaintance of the Marchant ladies, but she was as interested in them as they were in her and certainly knew them by sight. What was Revel doing, bringing a young unmarried lady here?

Her speaking eyes told Revel what she was thinking, but no sensible course occurred to him. "Hello, Mrs. Gardener," he said, trying for a casual air.

Mr. Marchant glanced up from the register to see who Esmée was speaking to—and found himself being stared at by his elder daughter. "Tess!" he exclaimed in a voice as hollow as a drum.

"Papa," she said coolly.

"We just stopped for tea," he said, with a guilty flush.

"Does one have to sign the register just to take tea?" she asked. "You had best sign, too, Revel. You have not introduced your friend, Papa," she said, turning her fulminating gaze on Mrs. Gardener.

Tess had often glimpsed this beauty from a distance. This was her first opportunity to study her

70

at firsthand, and she soon imagined a dozen flaws. The dark hair was dull, not shiny like her own. The cheeks were a little fuller than nature intended, and well rouged. She looked nearly as old as Mama, and not nearly as pretty. What did Papa see in her?

"As you must have guessed, this is my daughter," he said to Esmée. "I take it you already know Revel, my de—Mrs. Gardener."

Esmée smiled at Tess and said, "Revel and I are old friends, Lyle."

"Why don't we all have tea together?" Mr. Marchant suggested. He knew it was an appalling idea, but only wanted to put a decent face on the predicament.

"I have suddenly lost my appetite," his daughter said. "But don't let us detain you from whatever it was you had in mind."

"Tea! We are just having tea," Marchant said in an overly loud voice.

"I am sure Mama would have wanted me to give you her regards, if she had had any idea I would meet you here. And Dulcie, too," Tess said to her father.

"You must give them both my compliments, Tess. Sure you won't join us? They serve a very tasty tea here."

Tess looked at Mrs. Gardener. "So Revel tells me, Papa. I hope you enjoy it, but it does not appeal to me in the least. Good day."

She stalked out of the inn, with Revel making a hasty bow to the couple before darting out after her.

"What wretched timing!" Marchant said, trying to laugh it off. "I cannot imagine what brought Tess here at this time."

"Nor I, but I have a fair idea what brought Revel.

71

The lad has no reputation, but I should not have thought he would debauch a young girl like Tess."

"Debauch her? What are you talking about? Revel is my neighbor. I have known him forever."

"Ah, then it is to be a match. I am surprised the gossip is not circulating in town. Your daughter is to be congratulated."

A match sounded nearly as unlikely as a seduction. If it had been Dulcie, he would have been sure she was being taken advantage of. So young, and so pretty. But Tess? No, no one would try that sort of thing with her. If she had caught the interest of such an eligible *parti* as Revel, it would be a shame to scotch her chances by a scandal. He must be more discreet. In fact, he must drop Esmée. He was already becoming uneasy at her hints that she disliked these hole-in-the-wall assignations. What she had in mind was marriage. He had no intention of exchanging a beautiful, wealthy wife with a fine estate for a merely pretty nobody.

"All things considered, Esmée," he said, "perhaps we'll just have a quick cup of tea and run along back to Bath."

"You're right, Lyle. We must be more discreet in future. It would be a shame for your daughter to lose out on Revel. Perhaps we could take a holiday in London."

Mr. Marchant smiled impatiently and made noncommittal sounds as he led Esmée to a private parlor for tea.

Chapter Eight

Tess's long strides and stiff back told Revel she was angry as he accompanied her to his carriage. It was not until they were seated within that he saw the tears trickling silently down her cheeks. A man of experience could tell much about a lady by the way she cried. He had seen ladies howling in dismay as they covered their dry eyes with a handkerchief. He knew others females, especially actresses, who could turn on the waterworks at will and simulate every symptom of grief. Some watering pots were so softhearted, they cried buckets over a sentimental novel. Of course he had seen genuine tears, too, but he had never before seen tears course down a lady's cheeks while she sat like a statue, trying to pretend they were not there.

It was the lost and hurt look in Tess's eyes that betrayed the depth of her feelings. Oh, she was angry, too, but mostly she was just plain miserable. A man Marchant's age, a husband and father to boot, had no business carrying on with the muslin company. It created havoc in his family; it would bring the old fellow nothing but grief in the end, and for what? For a few hours of demeaning and uncomfortable companionship with a hussy. Ladies of pleasure were misnamed. They should be called ladies of discord. And the men who kept them were fools.

He noticed Tess turn her head away from him and unobtrusively wipe at her tears. He reached for her hand. "Do you need a shoulder to cry on?" he asked.

She shook her head. "A handkerchief would be welcome," she said, and held out her hand, still without looking at him. Revel took her chin in his fingers and turned her head to wipe at her tears. She resisted at first, but finally let him do it. "Your crying is nothing to be ashamed of, Tess," he said gently. Her mutinous glare told him pity was unwanted.

"I'm just so *angry* with him for hurting Mama," she scolded. "You can stop now, Revel. I am not usually one to spout tears on the least provocation. I don't know what came over me. I am sure I don't know what Papa sees in her."

The horses moved forward, and they sat a moment in silence, each busy with private thoughts. Revel tried to think of a way to soothe her and said, "Esmée is pretty, and he believes she is available without paying the ultimate price. When she begins hinting at marriage, he'll drop her."

"She is not half as pretty as Mama."

"I agree, but he has been admiring your mama's beauty any time these twenty-odd years. A man likes a change."

"I daresay Mama would have welcomed a few changes, too. Papa has had plenty of changes, I can tell you. I begin to think Mama ought to divorce him."

"It is you ladies who will suffer most if they do divorce," he cautioned.

74

Tess began to simmer down as the drive continued. "I should have told him Mama is seeing Lord James. That would have smartened him up. And instead of that, I have asked you to call Lord James off. I don't suppose you would ask your cousin to continue seeing her for a while?" She cast a hopeful look at her companion.

"He would be more apt to do it for you, I think. James showed some interest in yourself, Tess."

"I discouraged him! I was as stiff and dull as I could be on purpose to discourage him."

"That tells me you have already sensed his interest. But to be frank, his interest is in your dowry."

"I could not ask a favor of him! It would put me in his debt, and really he is not quite the thing, Revel."

"Why, thank you, Tess." Her eyebrows rose in surprise, and he explained. "I see you put me in a different category from James."

"One hears you do not seduce innocent maidens at least," she said. Revel's jaw fell open. "And besides, you don't find me attractive. Lord James does, or pretends he does. I wager it was my ten thousand he had in his eye all the while he was plying me with stale buns. So will you slip him the hint he can see Mama a few more times?"

"As I understood my job, I was only to lend you an air of impropriety," he reminded her. "Now you are adding a further duty—to make Mr. Marchant jealous."

"Are you hinting an employee is usually given some recompense for added duties?'

Revel leveled a bold smile on Tess. "Actually, an

employee is usually paid for performing *any* service. It is implicit in the word *employee.*"

"What a flat I am!" she exclaimed. "Turn the carriage about, Revel. We shall go back to the inn."

He frowned in confusion, but eventually thought he had made sense of her command, and he disliked it thoroughly. "I have no intention of registering at an inn with you. Your papa would come after me with a blunderbuss, demanding marriage."

"What on earth are you talking about? We are not going to register at the inn. I want to see how long Papa stays. He said he was just having tea."

"We have already been gone from your home for over an hour. Evans and Dulcie will be home by now. We cannot remain away any longer."

"Let us just draw off the side of the road and watch for his carriage. Just half an hour, Revel," she coaxed. "If you're afraid for your reputation, you can get out of the carriage and pretend you have a broken wheel, or some such thing."

"Oh, dandy! *I* stand in the perishing cold for half an hour while *you* wrap yourself in fur rugs."

"I thought you were going to help me!" she said accusingly.

"What is the point of it? We know perfectly well he won't be along for two hours."

"If they are only having tea, they won't be longer than half an hour. I should think you could spare half an hour in such an important cause." Her lower lip trembled and tears gathered in her eyes.

"Half an hour then," he said, and directed his groom to pull off at the next opportunity.

"Thank you, Revel." She smiled. "You are the most obliging creature in the world. I don't know why everyone says you are a model of selfishness.

You had best button up your coat as you are going to be out in the wind for half an hour."

"I shall stay in the carriage with you."

"Oh, dear. I don't think you should. If any of the Bath quizzes should see the carriage parked, what would they think? I would not want to tarnish your reputation," she added, with a quizzing smile.

Revel, snorting through his nostrils like an angry bull, drew his collar up around his ears and got out of the carriage. The wind whistled sharply about his ears. He explained the situation to his groom, and the two of them made a show of examining the left rear wheel. Every second carriage that passed by recognized Revel's rig and stopped to see if they could help. Many a curious eye gazed inside the carriage, where Tess was comfortably bundled up in the rug. In the end, Revel asked his groom to remove the left wheel, to lend an air of reality to the ruse.

He was just easing it off when Esmée's carriage came clipping along. It, too, drew to a halt, and Mr. Marchant offered Tess a drive home. Tess tossed her shoulders and said, "No, thank you," in accents that suggested she would sooner ride home in a hearse.

As soon as the tilbury was past, she opened the door of Revel's carriage to get out. The sudden shift of weight caused a lurch that sent the loosened wheel flying down the road. The rear of the carriage landed on the axel. A sickening snap told the story. The weight had broken the axel.

"Gracious, what is all the commotion?" Tess demanded. "We can go now, Revel. They were only having tea after all. What is the matter with the carriage? I almost fell getting out. What have you done?"

The wheel gained momentum as it reached an

incline in the road. John Groom looked at Revel, then went running after it.

"The axel is broken," Revel said grimly.

She gave a tsk of annoyance. "How did you manage to do that?"

"Never mind, Tess," he said through clenched lips.

"Will it take very long to fix? It's getting very cold in the carriage."

"Not so cold as it is out here."

"You're right," she said, shivering. "I shall wait inside. Do try to hurry, Revel. I am getting quite hungry."

Something in his fulminating gaze brought her complaints to a halt. She got in the carriage, and eventually a Good Samaritan stopped and offered to send out a wheeler. He also offered Tess and Revel a drive to Bath, which they gratefully accepted. Evening shadows were drawing in when they were at last deposited at the doorstep on Bartlett Street.

"Come on in for tea, Revel," Tess said. "You are shivering."

"I have a longish walk home, and there is no sign of a cab, of course, when you need one," he grumbled.

"Mama will lend you our carriage."

It was the hope of a drive home that got Revel into the house. He knew Mrs. Marchant would cut up stiff at their late return, but his chivalrous instincts were exhausted. Tess was more than able to take care of herself. Where had he got the idea she was a shy, biddable sort of girl? She was a managing hussy, and ungrateful into the bargain.

The couple were met with lamentations and scoldings. "Where on earth have you been, Tess?" her

mama demanded. "Dulcie has been home for over an hour. I thought you were all going out together."

"Revel's carriage broke down on the Bristol Road."

"What the devil were you doing on the Bristol Road?" she asked Revel. "You ought not to have taken Tess out of town, Lord Revel. When you suggested a drive, I thought you meant to Milsom Street. I will not have you carrying on with Tess."

"I'll tell you all about it later, Mama," Tess said, with a significant nod that hinted at great doings. "I have promised Revel a cup of tea, for he has been standing out in the cold for ages."

A shudder seized Revel's frame and he sneezed violently.

Mrs. Marchant took this for corroboration of Tess's strange story and schooled her anger to cool civility, but she made it perfectly clear to Lord Revel that he was not welcome at Bartlett Street unless his intentions were honest. Revel scowled at Tess in a way that did not in the least denote affection. The mother was on pins to learn what had happened, and was not tardy to call the carriage as soon as tea had been consumed.

The minute Revel was out the door, she turned to Tess. "What is it, my dear? You have seen Papa!"

"Yes!"

"I knew it. Where was he? Was he with her?"

Tess told the whole tale, assuring her mama that Esmée Gardener was not nearly so pretty as herself. "Her hair quite dull, and her suit not made in France. They were only having tea, so you must not worry yourself unduly. Papa asked for you and Dulcie."

"I hope you told him I am seeing Lord James."

"I forgot," Tess admitted.

"And there is not a hope of his seeing me tonight, for he never darkens the door of a play. You and Revel keep an eye out for him, wherever you are going. Where are you going tonight, my dear? You must take Dulcie. I quite insist you not leave the poor child sitting home alone again."

"Revel did not mention going out this evening, Mama."

"After all but compromising you this afternoon? Does he take you for a nobody? How dare he use you in this manner? I shall have your papa speak— Oh, it is *impossible* trying to rear daughters without a man to protect them."

"I was in no way compromised, Mama. It was an accident. Revel was not even in the carriage."

"I have it!" Mrs. Marchant exclaimed. "The concert! I have four tickets, for I thought when I bought the subscription that we would all be going as a family."

"I'll tell Dulcie."

"Yes, tell her. It is a shame to leave her sitting home again, but—"

"Oh, I thought Dulcie and I would go with you, Mama."

"No, no. You shall come with us. I shall send a note to Revel inviting him. It will remove the taint of impropriety for my being with James. The old quizzes will think Revel brought his cousin along and we are playing propriety for you youngsters. And Revel had better not make any excuses!"

"But what of the play you wanted to see?"

"I did not in the least want to see it. It was only Shakespeare. Lord James's idea of a lively evening," she added satirically.

Mrs. Marchant dashed off her note to Revel. A

reply was brought back by the footman bearing an unexceptionable excuse. Lord Revel regretted very much that he was in bed with the sniffles.

"Then I shall remain home with Dulcie," Tess said.

"Nothing of the sort. You shall both come with us. Folks must know by now that you are seeing Revel. I shall mention to a few friends that Lord James is taking Revel's place because he is ill."

"That won't make Papa jealous."

"Ninnyhammer. *He* will know the difference. And while we are talking about double-dealing, miss, why did you run off alone with Revel this afternoon? You have not explained *that* to my satisfaction."

Tess kept her tongue between her teeth and looked as guilty as she could, for she wanted her mother to worry about her. "We thought it would be more amusing to take the two carriages," she said.

"I swear I have hatched a pair of geese, with no more propriety than a couple of hurly-burly girls. Dulcie only seventeen, and jaunting about town alone with a gentleman. I'm sure I don't know what everyone will think."

"I expect they will think your daughters take after you, Mama," Tess said daringly.

To her dismay, her mama thought it a great joke and left in a rare good humor.

Tess saw her own notion of impropriety was sadly tame. What was it going to take to make Mama realize the danger of loose behavior?

Chapter Nine

The more Mr. Marchant thought about it, the more he realized he must return to his wife. He paid little heed to that silly letter from Lou's solicitor. She was only trying to frighten him. He had taken her running about here and there with Lord James Drake for an attempt to make him jealous—an attempt that had some success—but now he knew the whole. If Lord James was Revel's cousin, then obviously it all had to do with landing Revel for Tess.

He regretted losing Esmée. She was quite charming, in her way, but already her charms were beginning to pall. He was laying out a vast deal of money on his hotel and his outings with Esmée, but it was really the possibility of Tess attaching Revel that made up his mind. What a coup for the family! His daughter reigning as Countess Revel, at Revel Hall. Revel, like his father before him, was a bit of a high flyer himself, but his relatives would take it amiss that his bride's papa was not a saint. He could play the paragon for a few months, until the thing was accomplished.

Lyle Marchant did not consider himself a clever man, but if there was one thing he knew, it was women. And of all the women he had known, he knew his wife best. He knew she was still mad for him; he also knew she liked a little spectacle in her courting. He would not slip up to her door unseen some dark night, but execute the reconciliation in the full glare of the public eye.

He remembered that Lou had bought that subscription for four to the concert series, although she knew perfectly well that he loathed concerts. She did it to spite him. She would take the gels to the concert tonight. His empty seat would be there. He would walk down the aisle, bow, and make a pleading face. All eyes would be on them. Marchant had no aversion to a little playacting himself. Lou would give a show of indignation, then capitulate with one of her stage smiles. During the performance he would hold her hand and whisper sweet words into her ear. He would escort her and the gels to the tearoom and order the most lavish tea to be had. Pity the Lower Rooms did not serve champagne.

He could see, in his mind's eye, Lou's lips tremble in pleasure—while her eyes darted about the room to watch the crowd watching them. They would all go home together, and the thing would be done. He would mind his p's and q's until Tess was married. A spring wedding, very likely. He could be faithful that long. He really ought not to have taken up with anyone at Bath. Ladies were sentimental about such things.

He made a careful toilette and took a hansom cab to the Lower Rooms. He foresaw no difficulty in taking his seat. He knew it was near the front. Lou always bought the best seats in the house. He would just point out the empty seat to the page and say he was meeting his wife. He began scanning the front seats and soon spotted Dulcie. When he observed that there was no vacant seat nearby, he thought that Lou must have invited Revel to fill up the extra seat.

Marchant hired one of the last empty seats, near the back of the house, planning to meet his family at the intermission. Only the back of Lord James's head was visible, and that only by glimpses when the shifting of the audience allowed. It resembled Lord Revel's head in general outline and coloring. Not looking for any trickery, Mr. Marchant paid it very little heed. He was soon distracted by a full-bosomed redhead a few rows in front of him, and passed the first half of the concert without too much boredom. He also had time to tally his finances and figure out that he could afford a little gift for Lou; not the diamond bracelet she had been hinting for, but a shawl, perhaps. Sapphire blue, to match your eyes, he would say as he said on every occasion when blue cloth or feathers were presented in lieu of gemstones.

At intermission he stood up, waiting at his seat to join himself to Lou and the girls when they came down the aisle. He arranged a careful smile, suitably humble and hopeful and adoring. His attention was all on Lou. She was still a fine-looking woman when all was said and done. She outshone every other dame her age. He spared a glance to see how Tess and Revel were acting and his smile froze on his face. That wasn't Revel! It was Lord James! Lou was appearing in public with the scoundrel, and without Lord Revel to put a good complexion on it. Good God!

His next instinct was to hide, but before he managed to do it, he caught Tess's eye. She glared at him boldly, then began looking to see who he was with. He strode out into the aisle to show her he was alone. Lou had still not spotted him. He quickly left the concert room and went on out of the building. His spirits were in turmoil. It struck him like a kick in the stomach to see Lou with another man. And a demmed handsome one, when all was said and done. It was well known Lord James hadn't a feather to fly with, but he had a sort of inferior title and good connections.

Pride and anger lured him toward Esmée, to show Lou how little he cared. A second consideration told him this would only make matters worse. No, what he had to do was go humbly, hat in hand, and apologize. He would go that very night, after the concert, and make it up with her.

Tess found a moment at the intermission to tell her mother that Papa was there, alone. "He looked shocked when he saw you with Lord James, Mama."

"Good!" Mrs. Marchant crowed. "Let him see how *he* likes it."

With two ladies to flatter into compliance, Lord James was kept busy. Mrs. Marchant was too preoccupied to notice that Tess received fifty percent of his compliments, but Tess noticed, and was at pains to depress his attentions.

"You must try this cake, Miss Marchant," he said, passing Tess the plate.

"Perhaps Mama would like it," Tess said.

"What a thoughtful daughter you are!"

She gave him a scathing look, and meanwhile Dulcie took the last piece of plum cake and demolished it. It was about all the pleasure she got out of the evening. Mr. Evans was not there; indeed very few eligible gentlemen attended such dull scalds as the concert series.

Mr. Marchant was waiting across the street when his family arrived home. His blood boiled to see Lord James assist Lou from the carriage and hold on to her arm. And she laughing and flirting with him! When Lord James entered the house with the family, Mr. Marchant's face turned purple with vexation. Demmed jackanapes! Marchant paced to-and-fro, watching to time Lord James's exit. Eleven-fifteen slowly crawled on to eleven-thirty and eleven forty-five. Dash it, did the man plan to remain the night? Surely the girls were gone to bed by now. Lou was alone with him.

Marchant was about to cross the road and bound into the house when the door opened and Lord James came out. Lou stood at the door, smiling at him. She placed her white hand on his arm and spoke softly. At least they did not embrace. Marchant waited until James's carriage disappeared around the corner before crossing the street. He knocked once on the door and tried to open it. It was locked. He lifted the brass knocker and gave it a light tap.

"Don't answer the door yet, Crimshaw," Mrs. Marchant called. "Run along upstairs, girls. That will be your papa."

"Will you let him come home?" Dulcie asked hopefully.

"Why certainly, my dear—after he has suffered a few more days."

"Oh, Mama! Let him stay tonight."

"This is war, my dear. I shall not capitulate so easily. He would not be calling, were he not jealous of James. I shall let him stew a little longer."

"Mama is right," Tess said.

"But he might go back to Esmée," Dulcie wailed.

Her mother gave her a sad look. "That is a chance I must take. I do not want the old Lyle Marchant back, running around behind my back with every woman he meets. He must regain my respect and trust."

"And your love," Dulcie said.

"Foolish child. He already has it. That is what is causing all the mischief."

The girls ran upstairs, and Mrs. Marchant told Crimshaw to open the door. She sat, wearing an expression of mild interest, when he came in.

"Good evening, Lyle. What brings you at such an hour?" she asked.

"Lou!" he said, rushing forward eagerly. "I have missed you. You know well enough what brings me, sly boots."

She stopped his advance with a gimlet gaze. "Are your pockets to let?" she asked. "That is what usually brings your *affaires* to a halt. Odd, Esmée Gardener has not the reputation of an expensive woman."

"Tess told you. Now, Lou, that was nothing, I promise you." He edged onto the sofa, not daring to sit too close to her.

"Tess?" she asked, frowning as if in confusion. "Oh, I recall now. Tess did mention something about seeing you this afternoon. No, I was referring to general gossip."

"We were only having tea."

"Of course, Lyle," she said blandly, but her smile made a mockery of her agreement. "Now what was it you wanted to speak about?"

"I wanted to beg your forgiveness, and ask you to take me back," he announced, reaching for her

87

fingers. She pulled her hand away and twitched at her shawl.

"Oh, no, Lyle," she said, smiling sadly. "I am not ready to do that. Truth to tell, I enjoy being free of the shackles of marriage. There are so many amusing men about, when one begins to look for them. I begin to understand your chasing after women." She studied him a moment, then added, "One does get tired of the same old face, saying the same old things."

"This is Lord James's doing!" he declared, jumping to his feet.

"He is amusing," she allowed.

"The man hasn't a sou to his name."

"My dear Lyle, I do not have to marry for money. As you are very well aware, Papa arranged it so that Northbay is mine, and will become my son's when I die."

"I didn't marry you for money, Lou, if that is what you are implying. How could you? Don't you remember how happy we were in the old days?"

"Yes, Lyle, and I remember how unhappy I have been since those old days. I remember very well *why* I have been unhappy, too. You shan't break my heart again," she said, her voice trembling with emotion.

"My darling girl! I am through with all that."

"You will have to prove it, Lyle."

"I give you my word."

"Actions speak louder than words, Lyle. And now I shall retire. It was nice speaking to you."

"Wait! Don't go yet. We have so much to talk about. Tess and Revel . . ."

"I am not entirely happy with Revel's behavior," she said.

"Why, you cannot think he is trifling with her? He wouldn't dare," he said, squaring his shoulders and adopting a fierce expression.

His wife was unimpressed by his bluster. "Would he not, when her own father is a byword for profligacy and a divorce is in the offing? It is your behavior that gives him these ideas."

"I'll call the bleater out!"

"You will do nothing of the sort. That would completely ruin her chances, with Revel or anyone else. I don't say he has passed the bounds of propriety, but I shall keep a sharp eye on that young man."

"Tess would never let him misbehave."

"Oh, Tess! She has changed since you left, Lyle. I don't know what to do with the girl. It is very hard for a mother to keep grown daughters in check."

"It might help if you behaved properly yourself," he said. Concern lent an angry edge to his words. He knew at once he had made a grave tactical error.

Lou jumped to her feet, anger sparkling in her eyes. "You dare to accuse me of improper behavior, you—you aging Casanova. Get out of my house."

Lyle lifted his finger to shake under her nose. She batted it aside as she strode from the room. "Go, I say! Crimshaw, Mr. Marchant is leaving."

Crimshaw impassively handed Mr. Marchant his hat and gloves and held the door for him. Marchant rammed his hat on his head and stalked out into the night.

Aging Casanova. The words stung worse than blows. It was true, he was getting on. Half a century was no colt, but a well-aged nag. How unlike Lou to criticize him. Someone had got at her. Before long, he fingered Lord James as the culprit. The affair must be serious. Lou had never been one to carry on with gentlemen after she was married. Perhaps he had misread her—and she truly intended to be rid of him.

He went to his hotel, where he required a glass of ale to get up the stairs to his room. His lonely room. The four walls seemed to close in around him. If he had to look at that picture of a badly drawn horse leaping over the stream one more time, he would scream.

This matter required some deep scheming.

Chapter Ten

"Papa didn't stay very long," Dulcie said when her mama came pelting upstairs.

"He was behaving badly. I had to invite him to leave," Mrs. Marchant replied calmly, though her heart was pounding with excitement. Never before had she stood up to Lyle so bravely, and she was proud of herself.

"Did he want to stay?" Dulcie demanded.

"He came thinking to weasel his way back with empty promises. He knows my terms now. We shall see whether he respects his wife and family enough to behave himself. And speaking of family, Tess, you must either bring Revel up to scratch or turn him off. Your papa is spoiling for mischief there. Of course it is all jealousy over Lord James," she added, as this occurred to her.

"There is no question of bringing him up to scratch, Mama. Indeed I do not care for him in that way," Tess replied. "He is too much like Papa."

Mrs. Marchant stored up this leveler for her husband. "I never imagined he could be serious about you," her mama allowed. "What excuse does he give for calling?"

Thrown for a loss by the question, Tess said, "I

daresay his mama suggested it when I mentioned how little I was getting out."

"A fellow like that could destroy your reputation. You had best be busy the next time he calls."

"He did introduce me to Evans, and several other young gentlemen," Tess mentioned.

"Sly puss! Go on using him then, but no more of these late returns, or your papa will cause mischief."

"Will you see Lord James again?" Tess asked.

"Why would I not, when he is making your papa green with jealousy?" her mother replied, and left laughing.

"It's nice to see her in a good mood for a change," Tess said to her sister. But she had not discovered what she wanted to know. Had Revel dropped Lord James the hint he must continue calling a little longer?

"I think Lord James is a dead bore," Dulcie replied, and left in the sulks.

Cheered by her husband's efforts to win her, Mrs. Marchant took her daughters to Milsom Street the next morning and bought them all new finery. Neither Esmée Gardener nor Mr. Marchant was spotted. There was no assembly at either the Lower or the Upper Rooms that evening. Mrs. Marchant was edgy at the thought of spending a night at home without company. She wondered that James had not called. A moment later, she wondered that Revel had not called, and at last in a fit of boredom, she wondered that Mr. Evans had not called. Through her litany of names, the real question bedeviling her was why Lyle had not called.

All her wondering and worrying were soon at an end. Lord Revel came, bringing with him their evening's entertainment. His aunt, Lady Corbeil, was having an impromptu rout party that evening. The ladies must excuse the late invitations, but auntie had just arranged a scrambling little party for a few friends—about fifty in all. There would be dancing, cards for the older folks, and a midnight supper. All exceedingly informal.

"How very obliging of your aunt. I do not believe I have made Lady Corbeil's acquaintance," Mrs. Marchant said leadingly, for she wished to learn whether this invitation had come at Lord James's behest or Revel's. If the latter, then the lad was indeed becoming serious. Tess had mentioned the idea coming from Lady Revel, which suggested that dame was pushing for the match. Lou noticed that Revel exchanged a few sly smiles with Tess.

"Auntie mentioned she had not the pleasure of your acquaintance, but you will know several of her guests. Mama and I will be there, and Cousin James."

"To be sure. It sounds lovely, Revel. Your aunt may count on us," she said graciously, still wondering who had come up with the idea of asking them.

"I am delighted. No need to write a reply. I am delivering the cards and taking back a verbal answer. Perhaps you would like to come with me, Tess?" Revel suggested, as though an afterthought.

"She would like it of all things," Mrs. Marchant said. "We were bored to flinders, sitting here with nothing to do." Her eyes slid to Dulcie, who might well be included in this little outing. But then there was no saying that Mr. Evans might not call.

Seeing where she was looking, Revel said to Tess, "I should be leaving immediately."

Tess darted upstairs for her new bonnet and pelisse.

"Don't be late, dear," Mrs. Marchant called as Tess and Revel left. That was her only injunction. She would not like to offend Revel when it seemed Tess actually had a possibility of landing this excellent *parti*.

When the couple was seated in Revel's handsome carriage, Tess said, "Do you think you should be out all morning when you are recovering from the sniffles? Or was that all a hum?" No trace of illness hung about him. He looked remarkably healthy, though the wind might have given him those ruddy cheeks.

"It was only a chill. My valet threw me into a hot bath and a warm bed, comforted me with restorative liqueurs, and cured me. Beakins is a marvel. Better than a sawbones. Did you think I had forsaken you?" he teased.

"I thought you might have," she admitted, but without rancor. "My hope, when you refused Mama's invitation last night, was that you only wanted to avoid the concert. It was horrid, but Papa was there, and came to the house after." She told every detail she had gleaned from her mama. "So you see my campaign is bearing fruit," she finished, with a smile.

"*Your* campaign?" he demanded. "Surely you mean *our* campaign. Who twisted Aunt Corbeil's arm to have this party?"

"Do you mean you actually went to so much trouble for us, Revel? I am greatly impressed. You are entering into the spirit of the thing splendidly! I never expected such condescension, for in the usual

way you never go an inch out of your way for anyone."

"Thank you," he said in a weak voice. "When I
court a lady, I pull out all the stops and do it for-
tissimo. What sort of corsage would you like? Say
rosebuds. They are already ordered."

"Rosebuds are fine," she said dully. "I do not
agree with Mama that they are so common as to be
an insult. Truly I do not," she added when she saw
his lips firm in annoyance. "As it is only a small
rout party, I daresay most of the ladies will not
have any corsage at all. One would be expecting too
much to receive an orchid for a small rout."

"I'm glad you are so pleased, Tess."

"Have you had an opportunity to speak to Lord
James?" was her next question.

"His was the first card I delivered. He is aware
he may continue seeing your mama until further
notice. He is also aware his mature charms find no
favor with Mrs. Marchant's elder daughter."

"I hope you didn't tell him what I said!"

"I am not such a flat. I merely told him Tess was
a bothersome wench who bearled her poor escorts,
leading them to destroy their carriages and catch
cold standing in the raw wind."

Tess nodded in satisfaction. "A man his age
would be concerned about catching cold. Where are
we taking these invitations?"

"My footman is delivering all but yours and
Cousin James's."

"You lied to Mama?"

"Harsh words! I did not lie; I merely prevaricated. I told your mama I was delivering the cards,
not *all* the cards. I delivered yours and my cousin's."

"Where are we going then?"

"We shall drive into the country and find an inn for tea."

"You don't want to be seen on the strut with me," she said. It was not an accusation, but a simple statement. "I quite understand, Revel. Naturally someone who considers himself a dasher would not want to be seen publicly with such a dowd, though I am wearing a new bonnet, which you did not even mention."

Considers himself a dasher! The gall of the wench! "Very nice," he said perfunctorily. "Are you sure it's new? It looks like the one you wore yesterday."

"I always buy navy bonnets for winter, to match my pelisse. This one has a higher poke. You must have noticed."

"To be sure. At least a quarter of an inch higher. Which direction shall we head? Toward the Mendip Hills, or—"

"That's much too far. I cannot stay away so long."

He turned a curious eye on her. "Correct me if I am wrong, Tess, but was it not the plan that I help you misbehave? That you stay out longer than your mama likes, to bring her to a proper idea of chaperoning you and Dulcie?"

"That was the idea originally," she admitted, frowning. "It seems to be changing now. What I want most is for her to bring Papa to heel. If they are back together, then that hint of impropriety will be removed from the family. They will both chaperone Dulcie and me at the assemblies and so on. It achieves the same thing, really, only just by a slightly different method."

"That's fine for you, but it is not what I agreed to help you with."

She turned a wrathful face toward him. "Are you saying you would help me destroy my reputation, but you would not help me bring my parents back together? That is just what I might have expected from you, Revel. An enterprise must have a tinge of debauchery for you to be interested."

"The idea was never to destroy your reputation! It was all to be done privately, to worry your mother."

"Mama is worried enough. My aim now is to bring Papa home a reformed man."

"You might as well try to carry water in a sieve. A leopard of Marchant's age does not change his spots."

"Nor does one of your age, it seems. And furthermore, this bonnet is *nothing* like the one I wore yesterday," she added angrily. "Yesterday's bonnet did not have pink feathers."

Revel fell into a fit of the sulks and stared out the window. "I take it you want to go on the strut on Milsom Street?"

"Not at all. I won't disgrace you by being seen with me."

"No one would be foolish enough to take it for a romance."

"They might believe that at thirty you had begun to develop some common sense," she snipped.

"No, no, you have already assured me leopards do not change their spots." He pulled the drawstring and asked John Groom to direct the carriage to Milsom Street.

They dismounted, and Revel offered Tess his arm.

97

"Would you like to look at the bonnets?" he asked, trying to establish civil relations.

"I have just bought a new bonnet, even if *some* people don't appreciate it. It is freezing cold. Let us go to the library."

"The library!" he exclaimed. Libraries were for little old ladies, for retired clerics and vegetarians.

"You do know how to read, I suppose?"

"Only in English, French, Latin, and Greek. My Italian is a little rusty."

"You need not worry that the library shelves of Bath will hold a surfeit of Italian books."

They entered, and Tess strolled along, checking out the novels while Revel walked determinedly to the section of foreign books and took out Boccaccio's *Decameron* in the original, to show Tess there was at least one Italian book there.

Her fit of ill-humor evaporated when she found a new novel by Walter Scott, and they soon went back to Milsom Street, with Revel carrying the books.

"Shall we have a cup of tea at the Pump Room?" he suggested. "Not tea with cakes and sandwiches, but just a cup of tea to warm us?"

Revel admitted to himself, if not to Tess, that he had been behaving badly. He realized that he had enjoyed the little game of playing her suitor. It was unusual to be with a young lady who treated him so offhandedly. His flirts more usually hung on his every utterance. By helping her bring her parents together, however, he could still continue seeing her without the fear of raising marital expectations.

"About getting your parents together," he said. "It would be helpful if your father knew your mama was seeing Uncle James tonight."

She peered up from her cup. "Yes, but how will he find out? It is a private party."

"Someone would have to tell him."

"Mama does not let us call on him." She looked hopefully to Revel. "He is staying at the Pelican."

"Are you suggesting I—"

"Oh, no! No, indeed. It is just that there is no one else, Revel." She peered at him expectantly. "And it would be so *very* helpful if he could know about it."

"To drop in out of the blue and just announce my aunt is holding a party and he is not invited? Well, it would look odd. In fact, it would look demmed provocative."

"Yes, you must be more subtle than that," she agreed.

"I have not said I would go!"

"Oh, I thought when you spoke of the subtlety required, you were planning how to approach him. I am sure you could do it in a manner that did not provoke him. But I am not asking you to do it."

Her eyes were not only asking but demanding.

"Perhaps if I just loitered about the lobby until I chanced across him and mentioned it . . . It might take hours!"

She gave him an arch smile. "Or you could tell Esmée."

"I do not see Esmée."

"You said you parted friends."

"I'll loiter about the lobby of the Pelican," Revel said, defeated.

"Thank you, Revel," she said, and patted his hand for being such a good boy. "It must have been unpleasant for you to swallow your pride and admit you were behaving so shabbily. I appreciate it. Really you are not at all as bad as everyone says."

"I should like to know who this *everyone* is, who has such a poor idea of my character." His first spate of vexation changed to amusement as he watched her. "I take leave to tell you, Tess Marchant, you are a deal worse than society knows." She smiled her forgiveness. "Furthermore, the new bonnet is as like the old one as two peas in a pod. Why don't you buy a more dashing one? I have my reputation to consider."

"There is no hope of making a silk purse of this sow's ear, Revel. When we have got my parents together, you must find yourself a diamond of the first water, to reestablish your reputation to its usual heights."

She drew her book forward and opened it. Before long, she had begun reading, forgetting all about her escort.

Revel opened his Italian book. As he could not read it, he contented himself with looking at the pictures. A smile formed on his lips as he admired the sketches of full-bodied Italian temptresses. After ten minutes, Tess noticed what he was up to.

"The Italian comes back to you, does it?" she asked.

"Mmmm. Very interesting. Mind you, I do not grasp every word."

"A good thing a picture is worth a thousand words."

He noticed then that the page he was studying lacked any prose and hastily closed the book. "Some very fine artwork here, too. Titian, I believe."

"Very likely," she said, with a knowing laugh.

When their tea was finished Revel took Tess

home and drove to the Pelican. The taproom was preferable to lurking about the lobby. At five-thirty, he spotted Mr. Marchant coming in and strolled casually out to meet him. Revel seldom had trouble making conversation, but he knew this one was going to be rough going.

"Mr. Marchant," he said, feigning surprise. "Nice to see you again. Are you enjoying Bath?" He noticed straightaway that Mr. Marchant was not looking his usual dapper self. His face was drawn and his shoulders sagged.

"A cruel question, milord. I think you must know the misfortune that has befallen me."

"Tess mentioned it. I am very sorry . . ."

Marchant sighed wearily. "Tell her, Tess I mean, that it is all over with Mrs. Gardener. Tess will tell her mama. I have behaved like a fool, Revel. A man of my years should know better."

To agree, although he did agree, would sound surly. To disagree would encourage the fellow to continue on his foolish path. Revel made noncommittal harrumphs. Eager to get away, he wanted to deliver his message as soon as possible.

"I must be getting home," he said, glancing at his watch. "My aunt, Lady Corbeil, is having a little rout party this evening. Mama and myself will be there, and of course my uncle James. The Marchants are invited."

Marchant looked at him with interest. "That is very kind of you, lad. Lady Corbeil, eh? I don't know that I dare to attend. Lou might dislike it, but I will think about it. Very kind of you to drop by and invite me. Very kind."

Revel stood with his jaw slack, wondering how this awful misunderstanding had arisen. Yet it was only too easy to understand. He had been waiting at Marchant's hotel, and had come darting forward the moment he arrived to announce his aunt's party. What else was the poor man to think? Revel was too much a gentleman to rescind what had been taken for an invitation, yet for Marchant to turn up at the do uninvited was surely worse.

"I quite understand your reluctance," he said. "I shall be happy to— That is, I will deliver your regrets."

"No, it is not a firm refusal. I shall think about it. Lord James will be there, you say?"

"Yes, he is definitely attending."

"It could be awkward."

"Very awkward. Perhaps it would be best if I deliver your regrets."

"Still, a man must eat humble pie from time to time, when he has eaten forbidden sweets first. I shall attend, Lord Revel. You may count on my presence. Most obliging of you." He bowed and took his leave, while Lord Revel stood aghast at what he had done.

Chapter Eleven

Lyle Marchant was not a modest man, nor a pessimist. Yet neither his pride nor optimism quite convinced him that Lou was at the bottom of this invitation, much as he would have liked to believe it. It was pretty clear to him that young Revel's was the hand at work here. Revel wished to make an offer for Tess; he could not like to choose his bride from a scandal-ridden family. Therefore he was trying to patch the marriage up. He had done his best, poor fellow, but it was not within Revel's powers to keep Lady Corbeil's own kin away from her party. Lord James would be there, and Revel had come to warn him of it.

Demme, they were all civilized people. He would be a perfect pattern card of civility to all his potential in-laws, even including Lord James. And while he was about it, he would continue to pursue his wife. Lou could hardly throw a jug at his head at a polite party. He sent off his acceptance, which threw Lady Corbeil into quite a tizzy.

Revel knew he had failed miserably in his execution of Tess's errand. His instinct was to send Auntie Corbeil his own regrets and head off for London. Yet to send Tess and her mama off to that do without warning of the disaster awaiting them was unconscionable. He would go and confess to Tess, and let her and her mama decide what course to take.

He arrived at Bartlett Street just as the ladies were going abovestairs to dress. "That will be my corsage!" Tess exclaimed, and waited below till Crimshaw answered the door.

"Revel!" she said, and went rushing forward when she heard his voice.

"May I have a word with you, Tess?" he said, and herded her into the saloon. "The worst thing has happened."

She was disappointed to see no corsage. "If you are going to tell me you have the sniffles again, Revel, it will not fadge. And furthermore, that is not the worst thing that could happen."

"Sit down, my dear," he said, with a weak smile.

She remained standing and observed him suspiciously. "Did you speak to Papa?"

"Yes."

"Good. I assume from the hangdog look of you that you managed to turn the meeting into a disaster. Pray how did you do that? What happened?"

"I—" He stopped, conning his mind for the least damaging words to employ.

"Revel! You didn't *hit* him. . . ?"

"Good God, no. We had a friendly chat. The thing is, Tess, he somehow got the notion he is invited to the rout party, too, and he plans to attend."

She blinked and was silent a moment. "I don't see how he could think anything of the sort when he knows Mama is going with Lord James," she answered testily.

"She is not actually going with James."

"They will meet there. It amounts to the same thing. I am sure Papa will not come."

104

"I am sure he will," he said, and sank onto the edge of the sofa without realizing he did it.

"Did you invite him?"

"Not intentionally."

"Oh, Revel, you gudgeon! I should have known better than to use you on such a delicate errand."

He jumped to his feet. "Well, upon my word! This beats all the rest. I *told* you it would be impossible."

"You did not. We agreed you must use subtlety. How could you make such a botch of a simple errand? Really, Revel, I thought you were up to all the rigs. You are a complete clunch."

"I know it," he said simply.

Even the most wealthy, handsome, titled, and sought-after gentlemen carry at the bottom of their hearts some vestigial memory of childish incompetence. When the string is plucked, they revert to guilt and uncertainty. In Revel's case, it was only his mama who could stir these uncomfortable sensations; but Tess had unintentionally, and without her own awareness, discovered his secret. It is part and parcel of the situation that the ghost from the past must be appeased, to prove the wrongdoer's worth. "I am very sorry, Tess," he said humbly.

"You had best sit down, till we think what can be done about it."

They sat side by side on the sofa. "I don't suppose you could talk your mama into staying at home?" he suggested.

"You might as well ask a dog not to scratch his fleas. She has been looking forward to the party all day. Would Lord James agree—?"

"No point even asking him. He is the most selfish thing in nature."

"A family failing, no doubt," she said acidly. Revel's backbone arched at her tone. "Well, I must warn Mama, and just hope for the best. You must speak to Lord James—ask him not to dangle after Mama too assiduously. Can I trust you not to make a botch of it? Tell him Papa is an excellent shot."

"Cousin James has a few notches in his pistol," Revel replied.

"If this comes to a duel, Revel, it will be entirely your fault."

Revel's fit of guilt was fast evaporating as emotion gave way to reason. "You are the master planner, Tess. I am merely your aide-de-camp. We share the blame, but the major part is yours."

"I had thought men always took the blame for a lady's little peccadilloes. Or is that just *gentlemen*?"

"If you wish to use a lady's prerogatives, you should act like one. Your behavior throughout this entire ordeal has been that of a shrew."

She rose haughtily. "If we are sunk to calling names, there is nothing more to be said." She waited for him to recant, but he just glared. "You will speak to Lord James?" she asked, or commanded.

Revel stood up. "He might take heed, if the request came from you." He stopped and stood a moment, staring into the moldering flames of the grate. "By Jove, that might do it!"

"What do you mean?"

"You! Lord James will be delighted to have an excuse to dangle after you. He has no real interest in your mama since he learned Northbay is entailed."

"I don't want your horrid cousin dangling after me."

106

"You don't want a scandal or a duel, either. We must all make some sacrifices, Tess. I see a further benefit in this scheme as well."

"Well, I do not!"

"That is because you are selfishly thinking only of yourself. You must have noticed your mother—and your father, too, now I think of it—are beginning to harbor some idea that you and I are altar-bound. You promised to be the jilter," he reminded her. "Tonight could very well provide the basis for our pending quarrel."

"Who would believe I'd favor Lord James over you?"

"God knows you haven't shown any fondness for me."

"But he's old and poor. And besides, he is Mama's flirt."

"Do you want to avoid a duel or not?" he said, choosing the most menacing words he could find.

"Of course I do." She looked at him crossly. "Very well then. I shall pretend to receive his attentions with pleasure, but you must warn him it is all playacting. I don't want him dangling after me later."

"I'll call on him now. I must warn Aunt Corbeil as well. What a troublesome wench you are, Tess Marchant. I used to think you were one of those dull, well-behaved girls."

She glared. "I daresay that is why you never once, in all the years we have been neighbors, invited me to any of your parties."

"I seem to recall seeing you at our balls at Revel Hall."

"Yes, your balls, where you ask everyone, even the beadle. You never asked me to any of your private parties, when you had the smarts and swells from the city. Not that I would have accepted," she added hastily.

"That was remiss of me. I expect I thought you too slow, but I see you would have fit in remarkably well. You have given me a more proper appreciation for dullness and respectability these past few days. When this fracas is over, I mean to find me a pretty violet, blossoming unseen deep in the country, and marry her."

"Then leave her in the country, while you dash off to take your pleasures elsewhere."

"Precisely, but I shall take care to see she is placed in water and tended carefully." He bowed and left, feeling he had had the last word.

He did wonder, though, how it came he had not invited Tess to any of his private parties. How she would have enjoyed making fun of his friends. He would invite her to the next one, now that he was coming to know her better.

Over dinner, Tess told her mother and Dulcie the news. Expecting an outburst from her mama, Tess was amazed when Mrs. Marchant fell into a pensive silence. As is so often the case after a prolonged bout of marriage, Mr. and Mrs. Marchant thought alike in many matters. It didn't take the dame long to figure out that Revel was trying to bring herself and Lyle together. What reason could he possibly have except that he meant to offer for Tess?

"Revel thinks your father will attend?" she asked coolly.

"Yes. Do you think it wise for us to go, Mama?" Tess asked hopefully. Her mother's calm demeanor gave rise to the possibility of staying home.

"I hope we can both behave like decent parents in public. Of course we shall go, Tess. It is clear to me now that Revel arranged this whole party to bring your papa and I together, and of course to introduce you to his family. We must keep a solid front until you have him shackled."

"You are quite mistaken, Mama. Revel and I are only friends," she protested.

"I have often thought a marriage of convenience would suit you, Tess. And of course it is the only kind of marriage for a fellow like Revel. He would not want the inconvenience of being in love with his wife."

"It sounds horrid," Dulcie said.

"Goose! I used to feel the same way when I was a child, but I have come to see the error of my ways. Marrying for love is a grave error. Of course I would not force my daughters to marry where there was an actual aversion, but then you and Revel are good friends, Tess, so it will work out fine."

Tess saw that Lord James might prove useful after all. She could pretend to be in love with him, which would perhaps convince her mama to take her home to Northbay. But why did Mama think a marriage of convenience would suit her?

"I think a marriage of convenience sounds horrid, too," Tess said. "I would hate it of all things. To be married to Revel, while he ran about the countryside chasing girls." She would kill him, that's all.

"I do hope you are not falling in love with him, Tess," her mother said sharply. "There is nothing more likely to put him off."

"Of course I am not falling in love with him."

Yet she felt a prickling of hot anger when she thought of Revel chasing other girls. She was obliged to put it down to outraged morality. It was

109

morally wrong for married men to desert their wives and act as if they were still bachelors.

Before the ladies left, a whole bevy of corsages arrived, and the ladies fell on them in a glee. "How pretty!" Dulcie squealed. "I never had a corsage before. Mine must be from Mr. Evans. I didn't know he was invited."

Mrs. Marchant read the card and reached for the one orchid. The others were rosebuds. "They are not from Mr. Evans, dear. They are all from Lord Revel. Oh, the orchid is for you, Tess." She was annoyed, until she realized the significance of sending Tess the superior corsage. "And you say there is nothing between the pair of you! I swear you are full of surprises."

"It's purple," Tess said, looking at it askance. "It doesn't match my blue gown.

"Not purple, dear," Mrs. Marchant pointed out. "It is nearly white, just tinged with violet at the heart. You can slip upstairs and change your gown if you don't think it suits." Meanwhile she held the orchid up to her own pomona green gown, which it suited very well. "The white rosebuds would look well with your blue gown, Tess."

"Yes, I shall wear the white rosebuds," Tess said, and arranged them on her bodice. That would show Revel what she thought of his gift. She wore a scowl when they left the house, and was determined not to enjoy her evening one whit.

Chapter Twelve

"By Jove, I will be very happy to oblige Miss Marchant, Revel," Lord James said when Revel called to empty his budget. "This will make the lady smile on me more softly, eh?"

"I shouldn't count on that, James."

"Nor I." Lord James laughed. "I never met such a challenging lady. There is fire buried beneath the ice, you know. I like that. Her passion has been held in abeyance for too long. It needs only the proper fanning to flare into flame. It is not entirely cream-pot love that recommends Miss Marchant to me. I look forward to—"

Revel felt an unaccountable stab of anger. "To behaving with perfect propriety, cousin," he said brusquely. When had all this discovery of the fire beneath the ice taken place?

"Do I see discern a spark of green in your eyes, Revel?" Lord James teased. "This promises to be an even more interesting evening than you indicated."

"If you infer that I am dangling after Miss Marchant, you are quite mistaken. She is a friend and neighbor. I don't want you pestering her with unwanted attentions."

"If I sense they are truly unwanted, then naturally I shall desist. Paupers can be gentlemen, too. Very kind of you to drop by and warn me about Marchant. I say, you wouldn't have a few quid to spare? They are becoming a tad persistent at the hotel."

Revel left five pounds lighter in the pocket and with a growing annoyance with Tess Marchant. Now he would have to worry about James flirting with her, as well as Mrs. Marchant. His next stop was at Lady Corbeil's, to admit his blunder.

She said angrily, "How dare Marchant come here without an invitation? I shall tell my butler to turn him off."

"You forget, auntie, I invited him. Or he thinks I did. And the Marchants are close neighbors at Revel Hall."

"If he brings that revolting Gardener widow with him—"

"Oh, Lord! Don't say such things, auntie. This evening promises to be bad enough without that."

"I don't even know why I have invited Mrs. Marchant and her daughters. I do hope you are not planning to make misalliance with some country wench, Revel. Are the gels pretty?"

"Dulcie is quite a beauty," he said. "She takes after Mrs. Marchant in looks."

"But she is a very babe. Not even out."

"They tell me she will make her bows next spring."

"How about the elder daughter?"

"Rather handsome," he said grudgingly, "but a shrew. A managing, harping female."

Lady Corbeil could only conclude that Revel was entertaining a passing fancy for the pretty Dulcie. She had no real fear that anything would come of it. He usually found some entirely unsuitable lady to honor for the duration of his annual visit to Bath.

It was only to his mother that Revel could speak the whole truth about the imbroglio, and she, as usual, was not entirely sympathetic.

"No wonder Tess is annoyed with you," she said. "It is unlike you to be so woolly-tongued, Revel. How did you come to invite Marchant to Hettie's do?"

"He leapt to the wrong conclusion. Don't you rip up at me too, Mama. I am in everyone's black book. It will teach me to try to do anyone a favor. This evening promises to stand in memory as one of my darker hours."

She felt a weakening stab of love to see him so gloomy. "Things are never as bad as we think they are going to be. I shall insist that Marchant join my table for whist. He'll like that, and so shall I. He is the only player who can match me for skill. That will give you an hour's respite to flirt with the ladies."

"Truth to tell, I am tired of flirting with ladies, Mama. It is nothing but trouble."

"When a man is tired of flirting, it is a sure sign he is ready to settle down in marriage," his mama said, and peered for his reaction.

"That brings its own problems, *n'est-ce pas*? Look at the Marchants."

"Lyle Marchant is an old fool, dangling after girls at his age."

"I had no idea how many people got hurt in these affairs. All the Marchant ladies are suffering—as *you* must have suffered, Mama," he added, with a gentle smile.

"If a man don't plan to settle down, he should

113

make sure his wife don't love him. If you are beginning to find a conscience, Anthony, that is the best advice I can give you. Don't make a love match unless you mean to settle down, or you will break the lady's heart."

"I cannot conceive of making any other sort of match."

"Do you have a particular lady in your eye?" she asked hopefully. Tess Marchant would do very well.

"No," he said quickly. Almost too quickly . . .

"You will meet her one of these days. Ask Figgs to get my pelisse, Anthony."

Figgs's bulldog face peered around the doorjamb. "It's ready. Can you put a wiggle on? I am due at the Hart for a game of cards."

"Eavesdropping again, Figgs?" Revel said.

"Yus, and I have something to add to your mama's good advice, your lordship. If you sire any bastards, leave 'em provided for."

"And do not, under any circumstances, allow them into your home," Lady Revel added as Figgs threw her pelisse over her shoulders.

The party duly assembled that evening at Lady Corbeil's handsome mansion on Saint James Parade. Any hope that Mr. Marchant would do the proper thing and stay away was soon extinguished. He arrived, alone, not ten minutes after his family. Both Lord James and Revel had arrived early, to be on hand to divert disaster. Lord James had been directed to stay away from Mrs. Marchant, and as Tess remained with her mother, he had to stay away from her, too. It was only Revel who stood with the Marchant ladies, making nervous chatter while they all kept their real attention on the door.

Mrs. Marchant felt her heart flutter when Lyle

came in and looked around for her. He was still a handsome man, still virile and desirable. As soon as he found her, his gaze softened to adoration. It was Dulcie, ably abetted by Revel, who bridged the awkward moment. She darted forward to greet him.

"Papa! You came! I prayed that you would." She lowered her voice and said, "You *will* stand up with Mama, won't you?"

"I shall if she'll have me, and I'll have a set with you, too, miss. Don't you look fine as a star."

From the corner of his eye, he saw that Lou was in a receptive mood and allowed Dulcie to lead him forward.

"Good evening, Lou," he said nervously. "You are looking as lovely as ever. And Tess," he remembered to add.

Tess's "Good evening, Papa," Mrs. Marchant's "Good evening, Lyle," and Revel's "How nice that you could come" blended in a welcoming confusion.

They walked en masse toward the ballroom, where the sets were just forming. Mr. and Mrs. Marchant exchanged a nervous look. Mr. Marchant opened his lips, but before he could speak, Dulcie said, "Will you stand up with me first, Papa?"

The child meant well. Her fear was that her mother would refuse to stand up with her father, and she wanted to avoid such unpleasantness at all costs. She realized from the concerted glare of all present that she had blundered. "Unless *you* want to stand up with Papa first, Mama," she said apologetically.

"Nothing of the sort," Mrs. Marchant said, for she had no intention of being the first to capitulate.

Dulcie's father led her off to the dance floor. Mrs. Marchant began scanning the room for a sign of Lord James. If Lyle was ready to ignore her, she would not make a cake of herself by running after him. Revel saw her tightening lips and threw himself into the breach. "Mrs. Marchant, would you do me the honor?"

"Why, I thought you would want to stand up with Tess," she said.

"Tess has promised to save me the set of waltzes," he lied easily, and led Mrs. Marchant off to a square well removed from her husband's.

Lord James was not slow in pouncing forward to claim Tess. "I have been wanting to resume our acquaintance, after our delightful tea the other day," he said.

She looked him straight in the eye and replied, "I take it Lord Revel told you about my father's coming uninvited?"

"I am privy to the whole affair." He smiled conspiratorially. "Between us, we shall keep the peace, and bring him home to the bosom of his family. You look charming tonight, Miss Marchant. Gray becomes you."

"My gown is blue," she said.

"Gray—like your eyes—with just a soupçon of blue."

"I wish you would not flirt, Lord James."

"All part of our little evening's drama. No extra charge. An old bachelor like myself does not get many chances to flirt with such dashing ladies as yourself."

"That is news to me. From what Mama says, you flirt with any lady who will let you."

He laughed merrily. "That is why I am so good at it."

Lord James had uphill work courting Tess, but he did squeeze a few smiles from her. Revel, watching, was distressed to see her relax her guard. James was not ready to give up, but he was relieved when the music stopped and he could have a glass of wine in peace.

Revel contrived to bump into Dulcie and her papa at the set's end and exchanged partners. The Marchants stood together like strangers, exchanging a few trite nothings. After the ice had been broken, Marchant said, "I felt I ought to make an appearance. Is it possible Tess has nabbed Revel?"

"She might, if you can behave yourself and not give the family a disgust of us all with your carrying on."

"I have not seen hide nor hair of Mrs. Gardener since last night, Lou," he said earnestly.

"One swallow does not make a summer."

"It's a beginning. I have missed you so, Lou."

Fine talk, Mrs. Marchant thought, but talk doesn't butter the parsnips. "Of course, it is only a marriage of convenience Revel would have in mind," she said.

"That would suit our Tess, I think. She did not get your warm nature."

"No, she took after you in that respect."

Revel's dance with Dulcie fared better. Her artless conversation was all about bringing her parents back together. She saw it as a great sign that Mama had agreed to dance with Papa. Revel listened with every sympathy. It was really unconscionable of Marchant to put his family through such disgrace and pain.

Tess was put out that Revel did not have the second dance with her. She was not well pleased to see how attentively he listened to Dulcie and how soft his smiles were for her.

Her next partner was an aging general who insisted on reliving his glorious career in India, the highlight of which appeared to have been being locked up in the black hole of Calcutta. She was in no good humor when Revel led Dulcie off to the refreshment parlor at the dance's end. She told the general that her mama was particularly interested in India, and followed Revel to the refreshment parlor. She felt a pang of something hotter than mere annoyance to see Revel holding Dulcie's hand.

"You do think they will get back together?" Dulcie said, and Revel rashly promised to do everything in his power to bring it about. Dulcie's smile was not one jot short of adoration. "If anyone can do it, I'm sure you can, Lord Revel, she said.

Tess, hearing the tail end of their talk, gave Revel a disdainful look. "Robbing the cradle, Revel?" she asked.

"Where is Lord James?" was his reply.

"How should I know? I have been listening to a lecture on the black hole of Calcutta, and rather wishing I were there. Did your aunt not invite any *young* gentlemen to her rout?"

"She invited Lord Revel," Dulcie pointed out.

From the corner of her eye, Tess saw Lord James at the doorway and grimaced. "Oh, dear, he has found me. I have already stood up with him once. It is your turn, Dulcie. England expects every daughter to do her duty."

Dulcie smiled sweetly at Revel. "All right, but remember you are my partner for dinner, Lord Revel."

She allowed Lord James to lead her off; Lord James allowed himself a wistful look over his shoulder at his prime target.

"I hope you are not setting up as Dulcie's flirt," Tess said when the others had left.

"I had no idea she was such a charming girl."

"A violet, blushing unseen in the wilderness, in fact. If you think she would sit still for your sort of carrying on—"

"I hardly ever propose after just one dance. How'd it go with James?"

"He was all compliance, and trying very hard to amuse me. I don't know what it is about him that is so repellent, for he could not have been kinder. He reminds me a little of you." Revel's eyes widened in disbelief, and she hurried on. "Oh, I don't mean that you are repellent, Revel. I imagine he was terribly handsome like you when he was young. Handsome bachelors become rather seedy when they are past forty and becoming desperate. The flowery compliments that are pleasing from a young gentleman have grown threadbare. One senses the desperate effort to attract and is disgusted by it."

That "terribly handsome like you" lingered in his mind, to ease the sting of "seedy bachelors." "What flowery compliments did he insult you with, Tess?" he asked.

"When a man wants to compliment a lady's toilette, he might at least look to see what color gown she is wearing."

"And what corsage," Revel added, piercing her with a questioning look.

"Thank you for the orchid. I was never given one before. I was sorry it didn't match my gown. I thought you had already ordered rosebuds. I anticipated sickeningly sweet pink ones, like Dulcie's, and wore this blue gown, which makes me look

119

dowdy. I expect it was the pink ones you had ordered for me."

"Guilty, as charged. I wanted to atone for making a botch of speaking to your father and enlarged the order while I was about it."

"Mama was flattered. I'm sure you did your best in speaking to Papa, too. You couldn't help it if—"

He held up his hand to stop her. "Don't say it, Tess. I know I couldn't help being a gudgeon. There is no need to beat me over the head with my stupidity."

"I was going to say you couldn't help it if Papa ran away with the wrong idea. Really it is not going badly at all, and it is your contriving that has held disaster at bay."

Revel felt immensely flattered by this weak commendation. "Why, thank you, Tess."

"I only wish I didn't have to have dinner with Lord James. I would much rather be with you, so I could relax and enjoy myself." Familiarity had overcome her fear of Revel.

Two compliments in a row from this usually harping lady were almost more than he could credit. He scanned her words for a hidden insult, but could find none.

"Perhaps the four of us could be at the same table," he suggested.

She considered it a moment before replying. "No, we want to dilute the idea that there is anything between us—you and me, I mean. Mama is already speaking of my nabbing you as quite a settled thing."

Revel felt a spasm of alarm at this. "Perhaps you're right," he said, yet he was a little disappointed.

"Only think how horrid it would be if we were forced into getting married," she said, and shuddered to contemplate such a fate—while simultaneously peering for Revel's reaction.

"A fate worse than death," he agreed blandly, and left as soon as Mrs. Marchant and the general came to the refreshment parlor to have a glass of wine.

Soon it was time for dinner. Tess was forced to submit to Lord James's fawning attentions, and worse, to watch across the room as Dulcie flirted her way into Revel's heart. But at least her parents were seated at the same table and not arguing.

After dinner, Lady Revel made good her threat and got Mr. Marchant into the card parlor, where she fleeced him to the tune of four guineas. Tess had the promised set of waltzes with Revel, but the pleasure of it was stolen by her mother, who had the waltzes with Lord James.

"Why did you let him stand up with her for the waltzes?" Tess asked. "The cotillion or a country dance would not be so bad, but the waltz! It is practically indecent. I don't know how society allows it."

"Yet you and I are dancing in each other's arms without any fear of licentiousness," he pointed out.

"That's different. We are just friends."

Yet as she swirled to the insinuating rhythm, with Revel's arms enfolding her, Tess began to realize that she would like more than friendship from him.

"I hope we're more than friends, Tess," he said. She looked up and saw the laughter in his darkly shining eyes. "We are conspirators."

Friends, conspirators, but that was still not enough.

Chapter Thirteen

It was with a great sigh of relief that Tess thanked Lady Corbeil and went out to the carriage with her mother and Dulcie at the rout's end. The evening had not gone so badly after all. Barring having to stand up with Lord James twice, and Revel falling in love with Dulcie, it had been a success. Her parents had both behaved with more propriety than she had hoped.

"Is Papa coming back home?" was Dulcie's first eager question when they were in their carriage.

"Eventually," Mrs. Marchant replied, with satisfaction. "I shall keep him dangling a little longer. He must be cured entirely. Reforming him is such a wearing business that I should not want to ever have to do it again."

As they drove along the thinly populated streets, Dulcie said, "I think Papa's carriage is following us, Mama."

Mrs. Marchant thought so, too, and emitted a smug little laugh. "Much good it will do him."

When her own carriage drew up in front of the house on Bartlett Street, it was seen that the carriage behind theirs was not Mr. Marchant's, but Lord James's.

"What the deuce does he want?" Mrs. Marchant scowled.

She was not left long in doubt. Lord James pounced out and said, "I thought we might get our heads together for a planning session. Lord Revel has told me the whole story, Lou. Naturally I am eager to help in any way I can."

Mrs. Marchant was not entirely pleased at his eagerness to return her to her spouse, but as she needed him to make Lyle jealous for a few more days, she allowed him to come in for a cup of tea. "Ask Crimshaw to serve tea for four, Tess," she said, to give her daughters the hint they should remain belowstairs.

It occurred to Tess that Revel might be following his cousin, and she ordered tea for five. Revel did not come, however. While awaiting the tea, Lord James was voluble on plans to bring Mr. Marchant to heel.

"The thing is as good as done." He smiled merrily. "I saw Marchant peering round the corner of the card room when we were waltzing, Lou. He wanted to jump up and knock my head off. You have certainly won him back, and I am honored that I was of some use to you in the matter." His flashing eyes slid to Tess. "I only hope it does not give him an aversion to me," he added.

"I should not think it would matter much if it did," Dulcie said bluntly.

"Lord James means an aversion to the family," Mrs. Marchant interpreted, casting a brightly curious eye on James to see if he agreed. "He is referring to Tess and Revel."

"Tess and Revel?" Lord James exclaimed. The idea obviously came as a shock to him. Soon he decided it was a joke and laughed loudly. "I shouldn't count on Revel's being serious, Lou. He has more flirts than a dog has fleas."

This comparison hardly pleased Tess. She listened in growing anger while her mother said, "Has he said anything?"

"Nothing to indicate he is serious about Tess. He is not mature enough to appreciate her many sterling qualities," he added, bowing in Tess's direction.

"Then why is he trying to get Lyle and myself back together? I made sure he wanted the family respectable so he could marry Tess."

Lord James didn't believe for a minute that Revel was interested in Tess, but lest she was falling in love with Revel, it would be wise to squash that romance once and for all. "More likely he only wanted to make Esmée Gardener jealous," he invented. "He was pretty miffed when she gave him his congé. That was something new for him. I wager it amused him to use her new flirt's daughter to accomplish it."

"The wretch!" Mrs. Marchant gasped. "Really, this is the outside of enough. I never could credit that he wanted to marry you, Tess. You will not see Lord Revel again."

"I don't think Lord Revel would do that. He seemed very nice," Dulcie said.

Tess kept her thoughts to herself. Not by so much as a frown did she reveal her consternation. It was only too easy to believe it of Revel. Of course, he had lied to her about Esmée; she had heard him lie any number of times. He did it as well as a politician, with an innocent smile on his face. Why else would he have gone so far out of his way to oblige her? It seemed very unlikely, now that she considered it, that he had "accidentally" invited her father to

Lady Corbeil's rout. He had done it on purpose, to throw her parents back together. He must be very eager to resume relations with Esmée!

Tess pulled herself to attention and said, "I have told you before, Mama, Revel and I are only friends. I never had any idea he meant to offer for me."

"There, you have it from the lady's own lips," Lord James said. "Tess is not interested in Revel, so no harm is done." His smile beamed fondly on her, until she wanted to strike him.

The tea arrived, and Tess poured, to give her nervous fingers a job. When the knocker sounded again, every fiber of her body tensed. Revel! She prepared her blackest scowl, but it was not Lord Revel who was announced.

"Mr. Marchant," Crimshaw said. "Are you at home, madam?" he asked, lifting a brow in Lord James's direction.

"Show him in, Crimshaw," she replied very civilly.

Upon hearing her polite accents, Marchant hastened forward eagerly. His eyes spotted Lord James, comfortably ensconced beside Lou, and his temper flew into the treetops. He was not a patient man. To have to court his own wife was more than enough to put him out of curl. Guilt and fear added their weight to his frazzled nerves, and when he spoke, it was with a certain violence.

"So this is how you carry on when my back is turned!" he charged, stalking forward at a menacing gait.

Lord James bounced to his feet to defend the lady's honor. "Now see here! How dare you speak to Lou like that!"

"We are just having tea, Papa!" Dulcie exclaimed. She grabbed hold of Tess's fingers for comfort.

"Tea, is it!" Marchant said in a voice heavy with sarcasm, but as he looked around, he saw that this was indeed the case. And the girls were present, too. Embarrassment was a further goad to his exacerbated mood. "It is a fine thing when a man cannot enter his own house without seeing some jackanapes making up to his wife."

"Really, Mr. Marchant!" Lord James said. "I am a friend of the family." His sly eyes turned to Tess, daring her to refute it at such a time.

"Would you like a cup of tea, Papa?" Tess asked, glad she had had a cup brought for Revel. Why had he not come?

"No, I would not like a cup of tea. I would like to invite Lord James to step outside." Marchant's livid cheeks and indignant glare gave a hint of what he had in mind. It was to be a challenge, no less.

That look was familiar to Lord James. He had no fear of meeting any man on the dueling ground, but to kill the father of the heiress he hoped to marry was unthinkable.

"You quite misunderstand the matter, sir," he said gently. "When you and your wife have discussed this delicate matter in private, you will understand the innocence of our being occasionally seen together. It was merely an offer of friendship to a deeply unhappy lady. You have a rare jewel in Mrs. Marchant." He gazed deeply into her eyes. "I envy you, but I hope I am a gentleman. I do not aspire to steal another man's wife. Good night, Mr. Marchant."

He bowed and beat a hasty retreat while Marchant was still trying to figure out what the fellow

126

meant. As soon as he was gone, Marchant turned his wrath on his benighted lady.

"What is the meaning of this?" he demanded.

Lou rose up from the sofa, drawing her wrath about her like an outraged goddess and quite enjoying the melodrama. "How dare you come into my home and insult my friends—and *me*! Your association with lightskirts has made you unfit for decent company, Lyle. Remember, there are young ladies present."

Dulcie looked about for these people and realized they were herself and Tess. "Should we leave them alone?" she whispered. Tess looked uncertain, but decided they must remain, in case their mama needed protection.

"My association with lightskirts has made me feel very much at home in this house!" he shouted back. "The place is no better than a brothel. You are unfit to have the guardianship of my daughters—if they *are* my daughters!"

This was going a good deal too far. Without further ado, Lou picked up the closest vessel and threw it at his head. Fortunately her cup was empty. She missed her target by six inches, but the cup made a very satisfying clatter as it shattered against the grate.

"Don't ever set foot in this house again," she said in awful accents. "I shall inform Mr. Pargeter that you are not to see the girls, ever. Nor Henry, either. I will not have my innocent babes subjected to such lechery. Go to your rooms, girls. And take a good look at this—person—before you leave. You will not be seeing him again."

"Mama!" Dulcie wailed, and ran to pitch herself into her father's arms.

Marchant patted her head and closed his arms around her. He was more affected by Dulcie's tears than by his wife's playacting. Looking across the room, he noticed that even Tess, that cold-blooded woman, had a tear in her eyes. What had he done? He saw a long future of desolation, robbed of his family and Northbay.

"Lou, I didn't mean—"

She strode from the room, grabbing Tess by the hand and drawing her along with her. "Crimshaw, tell Miss Dulcie to come to bed at once. Mr. Marchant is just leaving. He is not to be admitted to this house again, if he is so ill-advised as to return."

"Oh, why did you *do* it, Papa?" Dulcie asked, lifting her tearstained face.

Marchant wiped her tears with his handkerchief and said gruffly, "Run along, my dear. This is not the end of it."

He left, before Crimshaw had to throw him out. His spirits were as low as they had ever been in his life. It was not until he was back in his lonely hotel room that the full iniquity of the situation occurred to him. He had gone, in all good faith, to make it up with his wife, and found her with another man. That was what it came down to in the end. *She* was with another man, and *he* was thrown out, castigated as a lecher. Calling him names in front of his innocent daughters. Oddly it was Tess's stern, sad face that stayed in his memory.

By God, if Lou didn't want him, there were plenty of women who did. He would show her.

At Bartlett Street, Henshaw put her mistress to bed with a dose of laudanum to calm her hysterics. Dulcie didn't want to sleep alone and curled up in Tess's bed, where she cried herself to sleep.

For Tess, sleep was impossible. Her best effort to reconcile her parents had brought disastrous results. A divorce was inevitable now. The whole family would be cast into that shady demimonde inhabited by such people as Mrs. Gardener. Where had she gone wrong? Everything had seemed so hopeful as they drove home from Lady Corbeil's party. Mama was in excellent spirits. If Lord James had not come to the house, she didn't doubt her father would be back home by now.

She never should have interfered. Especially she should not have accepted Revel's help. Knowing now why he had helped her, she looked for his hand in the most recent debacle. If he wanted Esmée back, he had outsmarted himself. Tess knew her father well enough to suspect he would return to Esmée. But then was there any real choice between Revel and her papa? Naturally Esmée would choose the younger, wealthier, and more handsome lord.

Yet she had jilted Revel. Lord James had said so, and she believed him. What reason had he to lie? Perhaps Esmée was only using Papa to make Revel jealous and bring him up to scratch? Esmée was not considered quite a fallen woman. She had still some shred of respectability. Revel knew Mrs. Gardener's terms. If he still wanted Esmée, he meant to marry her. And he had just used Tess to turn the tables on Esmée—to make her jealous and to pay off Papa.

He didn't care a groat that he had irreparably destroyed her parents' marriage in the process. What did he care for anything but himself? She agreed with her mother that she should not see Revel again. But if it fell out that she *did* see him, she would tell him exactly what she thought of him.

Chapter Fourteen

Mrs. Marchant came to the table the next morning restored to spirits by a night's sleep and to good looks by the wizardry of Henshaw.

"What ails you two?" she demanded of her daughters, who sat morosely chewing toast. "You look like a pair of hired mourners. I shall have Henshaw give you both a tonic."

"A tonic will not cure what ails us, Mama," Dulcie said.

"Perhaps a trip to the Pump Room will do the trick."

Dulcie looked so sullen that Mrs. Marchant laughed aloud. "Peagoose! I hope you did not take that little dustup last night seriously."

"Mama!" Tess exclaimed, more angry than shocked. "You are not implying you would take Papa back after what he said to you."

"Poor Lyle," she replied fondly. "He didn't mean a word of it. He found himself at point nonplus, and felt foolish for making a spectacle of himself in front of James, so he tried to bluster his way out of it. He will be utterly mortified by now. Your tears were a stroke of genius, Dulcie."

"Was it all pretending, then?" Tess asked.

"No indeed!" Dulcie assured her.

"Not *all*, my dear," Mrs. Marchant agreed. "I was truly annoyed with him at the time, but I would have had a rant even if I had not been. One needs a good grumble from time to time. It keeps the marriage lively. Lyle will be in the slough of despond by now. We shall visit the Pump Room this morning, girls. One can hardly affect a reconciliation in the middle of Milsom Street. Your papa will certainly take the waters this morning. We shall choose a corner table. I expect I shall weep a little, to show him how miserable I am. Remind me to take one of my new hankies, Dulcie." On this command, she took up her knife and fork and attacked her breakfast.

Dulcie was as easily restored to good spirits as her mama. It was only Tess who expressed her chagrin at this farce.

"Oh, pooh!" her mama said impatiently. "If you had a little more ingenuity about you, Tess, you would have hooked Revel by now, reeled him in and gaffed him. Plain girls have done as well before. You have had unlimited access to the greatest *parti* in all of England, and what use have you made of it? You ought to have been bawling and telling him how sad you feel, and how your life was over with the shame of it all. That would have allowed him to rescue you. Gentlemen like to play God, you must know. And what have you done instead? You let him kiss you the first evening he took you out. Dulcie is wiser. I noticed that sly puss making long faces at him last night. I wonder now if . . ."

"He was very sympathetic," Dulcie said musingly.

"You shall have your chance with him during your Season, my pet," her mama assured her. "I shall contrive another battle with your papa if need be, but it must be done quietly, for we do not want a scandal at such a time. Secrecy would be all to the good. Gentleman like to be in on a lady's secret."

Tess sat listening, keeping her thoughts to herself. Her first fit of exasperation with her mother had spread to include herself. This scheming and insincerity were horrid, yet she had an inkling the plan would work. Mama would indeed take Papa back. They would take Dulcie to London to make her bows. Revel had looked on Dulcie last night with a tenderness never shown to herself. With a whole Season to pitch them together, Mama might actually contrive a match. Tess had never given Revel any opportunity to be tender with her, to play the white knight and feel heroic.

She had engineered all the schemes herself, preventing him from displaying his own cleverness. She had ripped up at him and scolded, when she ought to have dissolved in tears on his shoulder. She had shoved him out of the carriage into the cold, when she ought to have slyly said he must not do such a thing, in case he took a chill. Then he would have insisted on doing it, and she could have fussed over him. Oh, she was a fool. He may have begun their flirtation with the intention of winning back Esmée, but if she had had a quarter of Mama's cunning, she could have changed his mind.

The ladies were soon rushing upstairs for their bonnets and pelisses. A merry mood prevailed in the carriage as Mrs. Marchant and Dulcie made plans for the great reconciliation.

"When I draw out my handkerchief and hold it to my eyes, Dulcie, you nip over to your papa's table. Do it furtively, mind, so he thinks you are disobeying me. Tell him how miserable I am, and how you think I might be talked around. He will ask what he should do. He will begin with letters and flowers and presents, I should think. You know the little diamond bracelet I have in my eye. But Lyle knows that himself. And you, Tess— Pray try not to look like Jehovah. Nothing is more likely to put Papa off than knowing you disapprove."

Stung by this remark, for Tess had decided to pitch herself into the game, she replied, "I don't know whether to disapprove of you both or to pity you."

"You may disapprove as much as you like, Tess, but save your pity for yourself," her mama said sharply. "You will certainly end up a spinster, the way you go on. I don't know why you must always take the pleasure out of every little bit of enjoyment that comes along. One would think you were weaned on a pickle. I never imagined I would have such a sour daughter."

"This is all so unnecessary and childish," Tess objected. "Why do you not just write Papa a note and tell him you want him back?"

"And give him the upper hand? My dear fool, that is no way to win a gentleman. You must make him suffer, so that he will appreciate you. I was as sweet as honey to your papa when we came to Bath, and you see the upshot of it. Tell him I am sorry indeed! Where is the fun in *that*?"

"*Fun?* I did not realize love was a game."

"That is where you made your first mistake," her mama said triumphantly.

A goodly crowd had gathered at the Pump Room by the time the Marchant ladies entered. They made one promenade of the room before choosing their corner table, to discover whether Mr. Marchant was there. He had not arrived yet, but they felt sure he would come and were prepared to wait.

It was as Mrs. Marchant was pouring their second cup of tea that Dulcie spotted him. "He is here, Mama!" she exclaimed quietly.

Mrs. Marchant hastily drew out one of her new lace-edged handkerchiefs, ready for her performance. "What is he doing? Does he see us?"

"Not yet. He is coming this way. There! He has spotted me now. Should I wave?"

"Just a sad smile, dear." Mrs. Marchant looked to see that Tess was not glowering. Far from it, the girl looked witless. She sat with her mouth open, staring stupidly. "Don't overdo your grief, Tess," she said.

Tess's lips moved, but no words came out. "What is it?" Mrs. Marchant demanded.

"Oh, dear!" Dulcie said weakly. "He is with Esmée Gardener, Mama. And they are coming this way."

"He wouldn't *dare* present that creature to me!"

"No, he is taking a seat across the way," Dulcie reported. "He cannot have seen us."

"He saw us," Tess said. "He looked right at me—and did not even nod. He chose that seat near us on purpose. He is just pretending he doesn't know we are here."

"How can we get out?" Mrs. Marchant asked, peering over the top of her handkerchief.

Tess examined the corner for a doorway in vain. "We can't. We have either to pass their table or stay until they leave."

Mrs. Marchant's face disappeared in a billow of linen and lace. A low moan came from the handkerchief. "Traitor! The treachery of it. I shall *never* forgive him for this. *Never!*"

Tears swelled in Dulcie's eyes, but Tess felt strangely detached. She had heard her mama's fatal declaration before, and seen her simulated grief. She felt that her mama did care for her papa, but not to the depths she pretended. That pretty handkerchief was hiding more annoyance than grief.

As this was a play, it required a second act. "It is a pity Lord James is not here, so we could march out on his arm," Tess said.

Her mother immediately looked up from her handkerchief. There were tears in her eyes, but there was also sharp interest at this notion. "The very thing! How can we get word to him?"

"It was just an idea, Mama." She was sorry she had given tongue to it. "Really a very poor one. There is no saying what the outcome would be. Papa might challenge him to a duel."

"My reputation is in tatters, my dear. A duel would hardly make any difference. To see him with that creature in such a public place as the Pump Room! The whole town is here. And his wife and family not ten yards away! He was always discreet before. This is as good as an announcement that our marriage is over."

"Surely his removing to the Pelican confirmed that," Tess pointed out.

"That was merely temporary, Tess. He has *really* done it now. He has hurt not only my tender feelings, but my pride. Call the waiter. I shall send a note to Lord James."

"No, really, Mama. That is a horrible idea," Tess said. "We shall just sit here and pretend we don't see them until they leave."

Dulcie kept staring at the table. Her eyes grew larger, and she suddenly announced, "He is giving

Mrs. Gardener something. What is it? It is in a blue case. Jewelry!"

"She doesn't take jewelry from men," Tess said.

"She is looking at it," Dulcie said. "She's taking it out."

Mrs. Marchant's curiosity soared to such dizzying heights that she overcame her pride and stared along with Dulcie. It was Mrs. Marchant who announced, "It is *my* diamond bracelet! He told me he could not afford it. Well, upon my word! I shall march down to Mr. Pargeter's office this instant and demand a divorce. He bought that bracelet with the income from Northbay."

"Perhaps he bought it with his own income from the Briars," Dulcie suggested doubtfully.

"No such a thing," her mother reported. "He paid Henry's tuition with that, and his tailor."

"This is the outside of enough," Tess said, every bit as angry as her mother. "To be buying his mistress diamonds with your money! I have a good mind to walk over there and demand that she hand them over."

"She's trying it on," Dulcie said, adding fuel to the flames.

This interesting show held the ladies spellbound for two minutes. They watched as Esmée Gardener wrapped the twinkling band of diamonds around her white wrist, then removed it. She examined it as it dangled from her fingers, turning it this way and that to catch the light. Sparkling prisms told the ladies it was genuine diamonds. Esmée then placed the bracelet back in the blue box, with some smiling words to Marchant. She did not put the box in her reticule, nor did Mr. Marchant take charge of it. It sat on the table between them, to be pushed aside when their tea and cakes arrived.

136

"He has ordered her the most expensive tea!" Dulcie exclaimed. "Look at all those cakes." For Dulcie, the most expensive tea was the last straw. Papa never ordered the most expensive tea for her. "Let us beckon the waiter and send for Lord James, Mama."

Tess, who still felt this was a wretched idea, crossed her fingers and said, "He won't be home. He mentioned he was riding this morning."

"Then we shall write to Lord Revel," Dulcie suggested.

"No!" Tess exclaimed. Her response was instinctive, but once it was out, she tried to find a reason for it. "He will not make Papa jealous, Dulcie," she said. "There is no point involving him in this business."

"He told me last night he would do anything in his power to help me . . . I mean us," she said, with a bashful little smile.

"There is nothing he can do, except escort us out. We need not bother him only for that. Let us just leave quietly. We need not pretend we have even seen them."

Dulcie's idea found some favor with Mrs. Marchant. "The very thing! But no, it will only inflame Revel's passion for Esmée to see her with your papa. You girls must each give me an arm. I could never make it out on my own steam. Let your father see to what depths he has reduced the mother of his children, with his carrying on. Has she taken the blue box yet, Dulcie?"

"It is still on the table, Mama."

"You see how little it means to her? I begged Lyle to buy that bracelet for me. Is it on the edge of the table? Might you pick it up as we pass?"

"No, it is behind the teapot," Dulcie said.

"Bother. I would not want you to scald yourself. We

137

shall just have this last piece of cake and leave. I could not possibly choke down a bite. You have it, Dulcie."

Dulcie passed it to Tess; Tess shoved it aside. "Let us leave now," she said. A terrible premonition of disaster was growing within her. This situation was fraught with too much chance for mischief. Her mama had no notion of propriety; her papa was purposely provoking a scene by bringing Esmée here and giving her the diamonds. How Esmée might react was unknown, but no good could be expected from such a wanton creature. To cap it off, Lord James might very well chance along at any moment, for he had said nothing about riding.

Tess began to gather up her mother's gloves and reticule, hoping that a quick exit might divert the disaster—or at least delay it until they were in their own saloon. She suspected that Papa was as eager as her mother to play out the climax and would invent some ruse to call at Bartlett Street. Tess was just handing Mrs. Marchant her gloves, and congratulating herself on her success, when Dulcie announced, "Here is Lord Revel, come to rescue us!"

Tess looked up and spotted Revel's crow black head and dancing blue eyes advancing toward them. Her heart sank down to her slippers, but it soon bounced back and began to flutter nervously. Here was her chance to try a little playacting with him and make a stab to win him. It was a wretched, underhanded way to win a husband, but if someone was going to win him by deceit, why not her?

Chapter Fifteen

Revel did not glance to his right as he walked hastily toward the Marchant ladies' table. "Good morning, ladies. I called at Bartlett Street and was told you had come here," he said, making a gallant bow. He could not help but notice he was greeted by what looked very like a clutch of mourners. "What has happened?" he asked, directing his words to Tess.

"Won't you join us, Revel?" she asked, still wearing that odd expression.

A death in the family was what jumped into his mind, only to be routed by their being in the Pump Room. He took up the empty seat beside Dulcie. She turned her lustrous blue eyes on him and reached for his hand. "The worst thing, Lord Revel. Papa is here with Mrs. Gardener. You must help us!"

Tess noticed Revel's fingers close comfortingly over Dulcie's. His eyes had stopped dancing and had grown tender with concern. "Shocking! I had hoped I would find you all *en famille*, things went so well last night."

"Lord James followed us home, and was there when Papa called," Dulcie said. "There was a terrible row. How I wished you were there to help us."

"If I had had the least idea, I would have been."

He included Mrs. Marchant and Tess in his apologetic glance. "How bad was it?"

"Papa asked him to step outside. It certainly would have been a duel, but Lord James left, and that is when things got worse. Mama ordered Papa to leave. And this morning Papa brought his mistress here."

"And gave her a diamond bracelet, right under our noses," Tess added. Revel glanced down the row of tables.

"Don't look!" Mrs. Marchant exclaimed. Revel hastily averted his eyes.

"I cannot believe Mrs. Gardener accepted diamonds from him," he said doubtfully. "Is it possible she went with him to select a gift for you, Mrs. Marchant, to make up for last night?"

"He had best not try that excuse! Lyle knew what diamonds I wanted. And he did not give them to me; he gave them to her. I saw her put them on with my own eyes."

"What is it you want me to do?" he asked uncertainly. A troublesome image of himself approaching Marchant's table and demanding an explanation darted into his head.

"Just lend us the dignity of your arm to get us out of here," the dame said in doleful accents. "There is nothing so humiliating as being caught without an escort at a time like this. A woman feels so vulnerable," she added, flapping her eyelashes from habit, for she had no personal interest in winning Revel.

Revel thought getting the ladies away from such a mischievous venue was an excellent idea and immediately rose to offer the wronged lady his arm. Before Tess knew what was happening, Dulcie had latched on to Revel's other arm, and she was left to tag along behind them. None of the three so much as glanced to Marchant's table as they hobbled out. Hidden by Revel's shoulder, Tess risked a glance and saw that her papa was squeezing Esmée's fingers. Thank goodness Mama had not seen that.

They had the honor of Revel's protection from prying eyes while they awaited their carriages. As his rig arrived first, they all piled into it—and also had the dignity of its crested door to mitigate their shame as they were driven home. This did much to lessen the odium in which Revel had been stewing the night before. Mrs. Marchant seemed to have forgotten that he had used her elder daughter so ill. Tess was much inclined to forgive him herself, at least until she had figured out the most romantic manner in which to fling it in his face.

Mrs. Marchant was helped from the carriage at her front door, propped up on either arm until she was inside. "Help me upstairs, Tess," she said in a weak voice. "Dulcie, give Lord Revel a glass of wine. So kind of you, milord. I don't know what we should have done without you."

When Tess had delivered her mama into Henshaw's keeping, Mrs. Marchant said, "No hurry to return below, Tess. Dulcie will put this meeting to good account if she has her wits about her."

"Are you forgetting how Revel used me, Mama? You said last night he only went out with me to make Esmée jealous."

"What has that to say to anything? His ruse failed. Esmée is going to marry your father, and Dulcie cannot be presented at Court. This is her chance to make a good match."

"Why Dulcie?" Tess demanded. "Why should *I* not make a match with Revel?"

"Poor Tess," her mama said sadly. "A lady has to strike swiftly with a fellow like Revel. You have got off on the wrong foot somehow. I doubted that even *I* could do anything in that direction when you came in all tousled the first night you were out with him. That was where you went astray, Tess. Had I known he was calling, I would have advised you. You must not hold yourself so cheap the next time you meet an eligible *parti*. I daresay Lord James—"

"I do not like Lord James. Nor Revel, either," she added in a fit of ill-humor.

"Pray do not go turning your sister against Revel, Tess, or she will end up a spinster like you."

"Perhaps I should put on my cap and chaperone them!" Tess said sarcastically.

"Did I not tell you to leave them alone, goose! How could he possibly make up to her with your Friday face glowering at them? Mind you, we do not want him acting too warm. Wait five minutes, then go downstairs. Dulcie cannot come to any grief in five minutes."

Tess whisked angrily out of the room. "A glass of brandy, Henshaw," Mrs. Marchant said to her dresser. "I shall not be downstairs for lunch today. If Lord James calls— But he is riding this morning. Perhaps I shall be able to walk by this afternoon. Lay out my mauve suit with the lace fichu."

Henshaw went straight to Tess's room, to find Tess pacing to-and-fro. "She didn't mean to hurt you," Henshaw said. "It is only her temper talking. What happened to set her off? She was so merry when she dressed this morning."

Tess told Henshaw the story. "What is this new

scheme of attaching Revel for Dulcie, Tess? I hoped you and he . . ."

"He is totally unsuitable for either of us, Henshaw," Tess said, and gave some details of the matter. "It is unconscionable of Mama to throw Dulcie at his head."

"What makes you think he was only using you to make Mrs. Gardener jealous?"

"Mama said—" Tess stopped and frowned.

Henshaw just looked. She never voiced any disparagement of her mistress, but her look spoke volumes. "Perhaps she was mistaken," she said discreetly. "Revel has not such a bad reputation as that. Those dashing fellows often make the best husbands. Better to sow their wild oats before marriage."

"He is like Papa. He has plenty of wild oats to last after marriage."

"I always thought a sensible lady could manage him," Henshaw said. Then she left to get the brandy and to lay out the mauve suit with the lace fichu.

Belowstairs Dulcie was testing her mettle on Revel. She had no real interest in him, but she was practicing to be an Incomparable, and this was her first real opportunity to hone her skills.

"Your arrival is all that saved us from utter disgrace, Lord Revel," she said, making big eyes at him.

Revel swallowed his amusement and replied, "All in a day's work for a corsair. I wonder what is keeping Tess."

"She is probably reading. She reads a great deal. What are we to do about Papa?"

"Time is the best healer."

She was disappointed in him. A corsair should not speak of time healing. That was *his* job. "My life is in

143

ruins," she said, staring bleakly into the grate. "I shall *never* get to London. I shall probably marry the groom, and end up a hag with a dozen children."

"Not you, Dulcie!" He smiled. "Marchant will come home, dragging his tail behind him."

"Not while Esmée holds him in her thrall." She cast a sapient look on Revel. "If only some other gentleman would divert her for a spell . . ." she said. "He would have to be top of the trees. A lord, handsome, rich."

Revel was not slow to grasp her meaning. "Esmée wants a husband, not a wealthy patron. I ought not to discuss such things with you, but as you presented the idea . . . Or did you mean that I should marry her?"

"Oh, no! You must not *marry* her. I wonder, though, since she accepted the diamond bracelet from Papa, if she would not accept a carte blanche from you, now that she is getting so old."

"She is only twenty-seven."

"*Only?* But that is ancient!"

"Three years younger than my ancient self," he pointed out.

"That's different. You are a man."

"What can be keeping Tess?" he asked again.

"Why do you keep harping on Tess?" Dulcie pouted. "Are you in love with her?"

"Don't be ridiculous. I merely want to discuss what should be done."

"We *are* discussing it."

"Is that what we're doing, minx? I rather thought you were sharpening your claws on me, in preparation for your coming Season."

"I shall never have a Season if you don't do something about this mess, Lord Revel."

He glanced impatiently at his watch. It occurred

to Revel that he should warn Cousin James of the gathering storm at Bartlett Street. James would want to distance himself from it all, or he might find himself involved in a duel. He also wanted to hear an intelligent account of what had happened after the rout last night.

He knew the Marchant ladies, with the exception of Tess, were given to melodrama. Ten minutes, and still she had not come. He concluded she was putting her mama to bed. Mrs. Marchant's hysterics might take an hour. He would go to see James and return after lunch.

"Tell Tess—"

"You are not leaving?" Dulcie exclaimed.

"I must go. Fear not, fair Dulcinea. I will not forsake you in your hour of need." He swept a playful bow and left.

When Tess returned a moment later, she did not know whether to be relieved or angry that he had left, but she knew she was disappointed. At least Dulcie had not ensnared him—although she was looking strangely smug.

"Where has Revel gone?" she asked.

"He didn't say, but you must not think he has deserted us, Tess. Before leaving, he said, 'Fear not, fair Dulcinea, I will not forsake you in your hour of need.' Was that not romantic?"

"Very romantic, but not very helpful," Tess retorted, and went to gather the mail. Northbay still had to be run, and this was not the moment to show Mama a lesson.

Fair Dulcinea indeed! Revel had never complimented *her*.

Chapter Sixteen

As Lord James Drake did not often receive a visit from his nephew, he was curious to learn what had brought Revel that morning.

"I would like an unembellished account of just what occurred last night at Bartlett Street, James," Revel said, accepting the glass of wine that was handed to him.

"High dramatics, my lad." Lord James laughed. "Were it not for my quick wits, that ass of a Marchant would have called me out."

"Was it really that bad? I made sure the ladies were exaggerating, as ladies are inclined to do."

"It was no exaggeration," Lord James replied, and gave a brief account of the interlude. "I shouldn't have minded knocking some sense into the old bleater, but then it would not do to strain relations with my future papa-in-law."

Revel smiled satirically at this notion. "I doubt you will make much headway in that direction. I shall save you the embarrassment of a refusal, and tell you quite frankly Tess is not interested."

"She could do worse," Lord James said, observing his nephew with a wary eye. "Tess would be Lady James. I take leave to tell you that impresses the mama, at least. Surprising how folks do like the title, even if it is only an honorary one. Of course from a worldly point of view, Miss Marchant could do better. Does she have someone else in mind?"

"She has not received an offer, to the best of my knowledge. I happen to know, however, that a certain titled gentleman of good family and fortune is . . . interested in her."

Lord James considered this a moment. "This paragon you describe could do a great deal better than our outspoken Miss Marchant."

Revel listened, unfazed. "There is something to be said for frankness, though—for knowing that a young lady actually means what she says. I find her conversation a refreshing change." Noticing his uncle's growing suspicion, he added, "And I expect her beau feels the same way."

Lord James rose and began pacing the room. "Demme, I thought I had a chance with Tess Marchant. Had I realized she was taken, I might have given myself the pleasure of putting a bullet through Marchant's shoulder, to show the old fool a lesson. She has not actually had an offer?"

"Not yet." Revel knew of old the capricious nature of his cousin. He felt things would ride more smoothly if James were out of town. "You would have better hunting in London," he suggested. "Even out of season, there are more heiresses there than anywhere else."

"I haven't a feather to fly with till quarter day," James said, peering sideways to see what he might weasel out of his nephew. Revel was certainly eager to see the last of him.

"My London house is not open, but I always keep a couple of servants there to tend it. You are welcome to rack and manger. I daresay my housekeeper would feed you," Revel said reluctantly. "You may use my season's ticket to Drury Lane."

"A kind offer, Revel, but I have a few accounts here at Bath that I cannot settle until quarter day. I wouldn't want to embarrass you by doing a flit."

"I do not take your antics so personally as all that, James. They have ceased to embarrass me. How much do you owe?"

Lord James mentioned a sum in excess of what he owed. Revel knew it was more than was required, but was so eager to be rid of James that he scribbled out a generous check. "There is a little something extra to see you settled in London," he said, fanning the check to dry the ink.

Lord James reached eagerly for it. "Very kind of you, Revel. I'll drop around and take my leave of your mama tomorrow."

Revel held on to the check. "Shall we say . . . today, James?"

"You are mighty eager to be rid of me."

"Your lesser antics do not disturb me. A duel, however, is something else. You have caused quite enough mischief for the present."

"Very well," Lord James said, and seized the check. "It must be nice to hold the cheese and the knife, Revel."

"You were left more than a competence, James. With a little more industry on your part, and a good deal less of gambling, you would be high in the stirrups. Whining does not become you. Your style is more dashing and devil-may-care. I shall take my leave now."

Revel rose and made a graceful bow. His uncle cast a malevolent glare on him and showed him to the door. Revel should be shown a lesson. It galled

Lord James to be led by an upstart nephew fifteen years his junior.

"You are welcome for the use of the house, and the money," Revel said pointedly.

"Did I forget to thank you, Revel? An oversight, I assure you." He closed the door, still without mentioning his gratitude.

Revel just gave a rueful shake of his head and left. Lord James was a hard man to like. The more you did for him, the more he resented it. But he would soon be gone. Revel turned his thoughts to other matters. Tess should be free of her mama by now. He wanted to learn what had happened after James left Bartlett Street last night. He glanced at his watch—nearly lunchtime. He'd eat at home and warn Mama not to give James any money. James would certainly try his hand at dunning her as well. She wouldn't be happy that James was being allowed to use the London house when she wasn't there. They'd have to warn the housekeeper to keep an eye on the silver.

At Bartlett Street, Mrs. Marchant made good her threat of taking lunch in her room. A morning locked up alone was more than enough to induce a case of the jitters. She wanted to be out around town, to see what was going on and to hear what was being said. That a small scandal might be included in her outing was no deterrent, but rather a goad.

She rang for Henshaw and began her preparations. An afternoon toilette did not last for two hours. She was ready to leave in thirty minutes, only to be struck by the notion that Lord James might call. His attendance was more necessary than ever now, to incite Lyle to jealousy. She found Tess and Dulcie in the saloon, discussing their situation.

"Get your bonnet, Dulcie. We're going out," she said.

"Oh, Mama! I do not feel like it," Tess said.

This was excellent. She had foreseen a battle to keep Tess at home, in case James called. "Then you need not come," the mama replied, feigning indifference.

"Do you think it wise to go out today?" Dulcie asked.

"Good gracious, the world does not stop wagging because your papa has taken a mistress," she said angrily. "Do I not still require silk stockings and gloves?"

"What will you do if we see them?" Dulcie asked.

There was no need to further identify "them." "Ladies do not hear lewd conversations, and they do not see lewd goings-on," Mrs. Marchant declared. "We shall stare through them as if they were not there."

While Dulcie ran upstairs for her bonnet and pelisse, Mrs. Marchant gave her elder daughter instructions. "If anyone calls, be sure you take a message, Tess. I have no engagement for this evening, if anyone should enquire."

"You mean Lord James?" Tess said, with an accusing look. "If he comes, I shall have Crimshaw tell him we are all out. I do not want to be alone with him."

"Naturally I do not expect you to entertain him alone. You must call Henshaw down. If he comes, he can leave a note telling me his plans. I shall get a reply back to him."

"You really should not go on seeing him, Mama."

150

"What should I do, Tess? Tell me from your vast experience of losing beaux. Should I run and hide my head because your papa is a rake?"

This discussion was cut short by Dulcie's return. The ladies left, and Tess told Crimshaw that if Lord James called, she was not at home, but he could leave a note if he wished.

It was not many minutes later when the door knocker sounded, and Tess flew to the farthest corner, in case Lord James got a peek into the saloon. Crimshaw had some difficulty finding her in the shadows when he came to announce Lord Revel.

"Send him in, Crimshaw," Tess said.

She was in some confusion as to how she should behave vis-à-vis Lord Revel. Anger and jealousy urged her to cut up at him. On the other hand, his having performed a useful function for the family that morning deserved thanks. Overriding both these thoughts was an overwhelming desire to make him fall in love with her. Perhaps if she used some of her mama's and Dulcie's wiles . . . Oh, dear, and she really ought not to meet him alone.

"Shall I ask Henshaw to come down?" Crimshaw enquired.

"It won't be necessary to disturb her. Lord Revel won't stay long," she said, blushing like a blue cow.

Crimshaw gave a mutinous look, but did as he was told. In seconds, Revel was shown in.

"Mama and Dulcie are out," Tess said. "I did not bother asking Henshaw down to accompany us."

"Good," he replied, and walked to the gloomy corner, where she stood. "Why are you hiding in the shadows, Tess?"

"I didn't know who was calling. I thought I might not want to be home."

"I shall take that as a compliment," he replied.

He took her hand and led her to the sofa. Tess knew that if she was ever to have her chance with Revel, this was it. They were alone, sitting side by side. She glanced shyly at him. "I want to thank you for helping us this morning, Revel. We felt so helpless, being caught in the Pump Room like that."

"I didn't do anything but walk you to the door. I daresay you would have handled the matter as well, or better, without me."

"Oh, no! Truly, I was at my wits' end. It was the answer to a prayer when you appeared."

"Doing it too brown, Tess." He laughed. "The reason I came . . . I want to hear from the horse's mouth just what happened last night after James left. Your mama and Dulcie were twittering so . . ."

Horse's mouth! It was hard to go on flattering him after this blunt speech, but she carried on gamely. "Things were not going too badly while Lord James was here. He is a complete hand, Revel. He said he was only a friend of the family, lending Mama his support at this difficult time. He praised her to the skies, and told Papa she was a rare jewel, or some such thing."

"That was well done of him."

"I was surprised at his handling the situation so well. It was after he left that things got really hot. Papa charged Mama with carrying on, and she said he was unfit for decent company. Papa said he felt quite at home in her house, for she was turning it into a brothel, which is another word for bawdy house, you must know. Well, of course you do . . ."

She came to a halt. Revel's lips twitched. "So I have heard. Then what?"

"Then he implied he was not our father, if you please. Well, really, I did not blame Mama in the least for throwing her teacup at him. I am only sorry she missed. It is clear at a glance *I* am his daughter at least, for everyone mentions the resemblance. And Dulcie has his nose, though she got Mama's eyes and hair and manner."

She recalled that she meant to borrow that manner, and added in a sweet accent, far removed from her normal voice, "Oh, it was horrid, Revel. If only you had been here I'm sure you could have prevented Mama from telling him never to darken her door again."

"Cut line, Tess," he said curtly. "I did not come here to have the butter boat dumped over me. Your main charm has always been your lack of wiles. Don't insult my intelligence by playing off these stale tricks."

"What intelligence?" she snapped. Her eyes flashed dangerously, and her fawning expression firmed to vexation.

"That is more like it. Then what did your father do?"

"He left, and obviously ran straight to Esmée. How else did she earn that diamond bracelet that was dangling from her wrist this morning?"

"That diamond bracelet— There is something amiss there. She would never take diamonds from me."

"Your powers of persuasion must be sadly lacking if you cannot even get a lightskirt to accept diamonds," she snipped.

"I have told you, what the lady wants is a golden band. Esmée is not a lightskirt, precisely."

"What would you call a woman who can be had outside of marriage?" she demanded.

"Very obliging," he answered promptly. "But until she takes payment, she ain't a lightskirt."

"This is mere playing with words."

"A game for which you are ill-equipped," he teased.

"A woman of that sort is a lightskirt, whatever you choose to call her."

"You forget Esmée is a widow. That gives her some latitude in her dealings with gentlemen."

"So it seems. About the bracelet, I can only conclude that Papa has offered her marriage, after the divorce comes through."

Revel could not place any other construction on it, either, and his anger showed. "This is intolerable!"

"It seems you will have to up the ante, Revel. If you want her back, you must put your diamonds in your pocket and buy the golden band."

"Don't speak like an idiot. I expect more sense from you," he said gruffly.

From horse to idiot! Her patience was at an end. "I am finished with being an idiot. You have had your little game, Revel. You have paid Papa off for stealing your flirt by using me to make Esmée jealous. I wondered at your sudden fit of compliance, when you never stirred a finger to help anyone before in your life."

Revel's shoulders tensed. His expression froze to disdain, and he said loftily, "Are you quite through, Tess?"

"Not quite. As you deem me capable of handling unseemly matters, I shall give you a little advice. The lady obviously means business. I daresay Esmée would prefer a well-inlaid lord, even if he has a tarnished reputation, to an older divorced man with only a modest estate in York. If you want her, you had best get a move on, or Papa will beat you to her."

His expression thawed to simple annoyance, then further melted to a smile. "Now that is a performance worthy of you, shrew," he said softly. "I thank you for your advice." He rose. "It won't be necessary for you to hide in the corner again. James won't be calling."

"How do you know? Where is he? Has he left?"

"Not yet, but he will be leaving soon."

"Did you send him away? I don't understand, Revel. We were counting on him—"

His eyes narrowed. "May I know for what?"

Tess lifted her chin. "Don't worry. It does not concern you and Esmée."

Revel made a bow and hastened out to his carriage. "Mrs. Gardener's flat," he called to his groom.

Chapter Seventeen

"Lord James did not call," Tess said when her mama and Dulcie returned. She feared this news would put Mama in one of her moods, but it was no such a thing.

"Did he not, dear? Then you might as well have come with us," Mrs. Marchant replied airily.

Tess looked to her sister for an explanation. "We met Esmée," Dulcie announced, smiling from ear to ear.

"Not with Papa, I take it?"

"She was with Lord Revel," Mrs. Marchant said, and went off into joyous hoots of laughter.

Tess stood like a statue. This was *her* fault. *She* had advised Revel to go back to Esmée, but she had not thought he would follow her advice with such unholy promptitude. He must truly be in love with that scarlet woman.

Mrs. Marchant asked Crimshaw to bring tea, and gathered her daughters around her in the saloon for a good cose.

"It is famous!" she crowed. "Did I not say all along, Tess, that Revel was only using you to make Esmée jealous? The young fool has offered her marriage, certainly. His mama will hit the roof."

"What about Papa?" Tess asked in a quavering

voice, though at that moment she did not care if she ever saw him again. It was the image of Revel with Esmée that had undone her.

"The vibrato is slightly overdone, my dear, but that was a very good attempt at having feelings," Mrs. Marchant said, and gave Tess's hand a maternal pat, then went off into further gales of laughter. "Now you will see your papa come trotting home."

"You will take him back this time, Mama?" Dulcie urged. "*Please*, do it. Don't let him fall into a hobble with some other lady."

"If he has learned his lesson," Mrs. Marchant said, with a loving gleam in one eye and a wily glint in the other. "And an expensive lesson it was. That diamond bracelet cost fifty guineas."

"Did you see Papa at all?" Tess asked.

"I fancy he was hiding his shame at the Pelican," her mama replied. "If Lord James calls, I shall not go out."

Tess knew that Lord James was leaving. She ought to tell her mother about Revel's call, but she felt a peculiar reluctance to mention his name. A strange lump was growing in her throat. He had gone back to Esmée. Her best efforts to ingratiate him had failed. He had called her a horse and an idiot.

"Why are you looking so glum?" Mrs. Marchant demanded. "I should think you would be happy, child."

"She's blue because she has lost Lord Revel," Dulcie said. "I don't believe he loves Esmée at all. I think it is just a ruse. In fact, I asked him to do it."

"He didn't do it for you! *I* suggested it, too," Tess

replied hotly. No one thought to enquire when she made this request.

"Ninnies." Their mother laughed. "As though he would go an inch out of his way to oblige either of you hussies. It is famous that the great Lord Revel has been caught by a lightskirt, but really I cannot like to think of Esmée living so close to Lyle at home."

"Lord Revel won't marry her, Mama," Dulcie repeated.

"You are probably right. He has offered her carte blanche—an allowance, a flat in London, her own carriage and team, and all the rest of it. If she is wise, she will snap at it, for she is getting pretty long in the tooth. Is that not what you said, Tess, when you saw her at the George and Dragon?"

"Yes, I did not find her at all attractive." That description had been designed to please her mama. What Tess was seeing in her mind's eyes was an extremely elegant lady with a flashing smile and clever eyes. Of course Revel was in love with her. What gentleman with the use of his wits would not be?

"I wonder if she has formally given your papa his congé," was Mrs. Marchant's next concern. "If she is at all nice, she would have let him know before appearing in public with Lord Revel. I wager your papa has been stewing in his shame for hours." Her gleeful smile showed total satisfaction with this.

The tea came, and the conversation continued, covering the same ground, with slight variations. The pot was still warm when the knocker sounded, bringing conversation to a halt.

A chilly breeze and the echo of a muted conversation came to the ladies from the open doorway, while they all strained their ears to discover if the voice was Mr. Marchant's. Soon Crimshaw came to put them out of their suspense.

"A note for you, madam," he said, handing Mrs. Marchant a letter.

Her cheeks blanched, throwing into prominence two spots of pink rouge so carefully applied that it looked almost natural. She opened the note with trembling fingers. "It is from your papa," she announced in hushed accents. Her staring eyes devoured the page greedily.

"Will there be a reply, madam?" Crimshaw enquired. "The footman is waiting."

"Hush, Crimshaw," she said, without glancing up from the page. After a cursory reading, she looked up. A frown pleated her brow. The apology was abject enough to please her; the pleading for mercy and another chance were all that she could wish. What was lacking was any mention of a diamond bracelet. Did Lyle think he had only to hang his head and tug his forelock and all would be well? She could hold out until the diamonds were forthcoming, now that Revel had removed the threat of Mrs. Gardener.

"Madam?" Crimshaw repeated.

"Tell the footman— No, I had best write a note. There is no counting on servants to deliver a message properly."

She strode to the writing desk in the corner and drew forth a sheet of writing paper. What she wished to convey was that talk was cheap. Where was the bracelet? After some thought, she wrote:

Dear Lyle:

Your sentiments do you credit, but until I see some tangible proof of your intentions, I must re-

159

strain my eagerness to welcome you into the bosom of your family. I shall be at home this evening.

She signed it, folded it up, and handed it to Crimshaw, who took it to the footman.

"Is Papa coming home?" Dulcie asked eagerly.

"I rather think we shall see him this evening." Her mama smiled. Lyle had the afternoon to raise the wind and make the purchase.

Tess cleared her throat and said, "Does the note say anything about Revel, Mama? Has he made any sort of offer for Esmée?"

"There is not a word about Revel. We shall not tease your papa about Revel beating him out." Her eyes narrowed, and she continued on bemusedly, "But certainly that is why Esmée dumped your papa."

"Do you mean Papa is only coming back to us because Esmée won't have him?" Dulcie demanded.

"It does not do to look too closely into some dealings, my dear. Your papa says he did not love Mrs. Gardener, and did not offer for her. I shall believe him when—" Two pairs of curious young eyes regarded her expectantly.

"He did not offer you a bracelet," Dulcie said. "Really, Mama, I don't think you should let that stand in the way of a reconciliation."

"It is not only the bracelet, goose! He must prove he loves *me* more than he loves *her*."

"Have you considered that his pockets may be to let?" Tess said. "He would have offered you one if he had the money."

"Does he not have a diamond tiepin as big as a gooseberry? What is to prevent him from hawking it?"

160

"It belonged to his father, Mama!" Tess said, shocked.

"If he loves me, he will arrange the dibs somehow." On this firm speech Mrs. Marchant rose and went to her room.

Tess looked doubtful. "Papa will never sell his father's tiepin. I don't think Mama should ask it of him."

"I daresay he could borrow the money, if he is short," Dulcie said.

"Yes, his credit is good. He will arrange the loan this afternoon and come this evening with the bracelet. But I still think it wrong of Mama to tie her acceptance of him to a set of diamonds, like a lightskirt."

"Just as long as he comes home," Dulcie said, and went off to continue her novel.

At the Pelican, Mr. Marchant was not slow to interpret his wife's letter. His pockets were indeed to let, but selling his keepsake of his father never so much as entered his head. He had been shocked to learn from Mrs. Gardener's butler, when he called that afternoon, that she was out with Lord Revel. As she was taking up with her old beau, she would naturally return the bracelet. He would give it to Lou, and all would be well.

The last thing he wanted was to call on Esmée and find Revel in her saloon. He wrote a note asking when it would be convenient for him to call and pick up the bracelet, as he understood from her butler that she was seeing another gentleman.

With a sly smile, Mrs. Gardener wrote back:

A gentleman does not demand the return of a gift. Shall we say, for services already rendered? Best regards, E.G.

She had made other arrangements for the disposal of the bracelet. Let Lyle Marchant stew for a few hours, old fool! It would teach him a much needed lesson. She forgot Lyle as soon as she sent the note off. After Lord Revel's unexpected visit, she had more interesting things to consider. If Revel were right, she would soon be shaking the dust of this town from her slippers.

Mr. Marchant was thrown into terrible uncertainty by the note. Like any childish, thoroughly selfish person, he was soon convinced he had been hard done by. Robbery hardly seemed too harsh a word for Esmée's stunt, and he did not mean to tolerate it. He would march to her apartment and demand the bracelet back. But first he would have a beefsteak, as it was close to dinnertime, and a bottle of wine to buck up his spirits.

As he ate his solitary dinner, he reviewed his past and came to the conclusion that a married man his age was a fool to trifle with the muslin company. Esmée had cost him a monkey, and put his marriage in jeopardy to boot. It had been a happy marriage, barring a few arguments. His mind wandered to young Henry. He would be growing up one of these days. A man should not show his son a poor example. Yes, all things considered, it was time to reform.

After dinner he made a careful toilette, went out into the street, and hailed a hansom cab to take him to Mrs. Gardener's flat. There was another advantage to reconciliation. He would have the use of his carriage again. He disliked hiring cabs, like a commoner. It was unbecoming to Mr. Marchant, of Northbay, Wiltshire, and the Briars in York.

Lord Revel also had a busy afternoon. He had to

see Esmée and feel her out on her view of removing to London. With the lure of a possible marriage and a title, and the actual promise of a diamond bracelet, the lady was not averse. Then he had to buy a diamond bracelet slightly superior to that Marchant had given Esmée. He dashed home to catch Lord James just as he was leaving Lady Revel's saloon, which saved him a trip to his cousin's hotel.

They had a word at the front doorway. "James, I am happy I caught you before you left. I have just been speaking to an old friend who will be off to London very soon. She has few acquaintances there. I told her I would ask you to call."

"Her?" James asked, honing in on the most interesting word.

"Mrs. Gardener. She has rooms in Bridewell Lane. A charming lady."

"Marchant's mistress, and your ex?" Lord James exclaimed, offended. "A man in my position cannot afford to keep a lightskirt."

"You misread the lady's character. She is no lightskirt, James," Revel said, feigning shock. "She is a respectable widow. Bath is no city for a lovely young widow. Her every gentleman friend is accused of keeping her. Good God, as though Esmée Gardener needed to be kept. Her late husband left her well to grass. Something in the neighborhood of twenty thousand."

It was like dangling a meaty bone before a hungry dog. "I daresay I could find time to call, if it would please you," Lord James said.

"It would please me exceedingly," Revel replied.

"Where will she be staying?"

"She did not have an address yet, when I spoke

to her. Shall I give her yours, so that she may drop you a line when she arrives?"

"Certainly, Revel." James was unaccustomed to receiving gifts—and tended to suspect any such offering of Grecian tricks. He sensed some chicanery in Revel's dancing eyes. "I never heard Esmée Gardener was a nabob," he said doubtfully.

"She takes care that it is not bruited about . . . draws the wrong sort, you know. She is not interested in a common fortune hunter."

James was cunning enough to read into this that the lady might not be averse to an aristocratic one. He went back to the hotel to oversee his packing. Visions of twenty thousand pounds whirled through his brain. And the lady was not an antidote by any means. In fact, she put any other lady in Bath to the blush, and could even hold her own in London. Eagerness to begin paying court writhed within him. Why wait until she was in London? The fortune hunters would be knee deep within days. Why not beat the rush and drop in on her this evening? He could leave for London tomorrow. What was the address Revel had mentioned? Bridewell Lane—a promising address!

He drove to his hotel and made a careful toilette, then called for his carriage and directed his groom to Bridewell Lane.

At Royal Crescent, Lord Revel took dinner with his mama. They spoke of Lord James's remove to London and the probable depredations on their silver and valuable bibelots. "Actually, I expect he will not be there long," Revel said, biting back a smile.

"I cannot imagine why you offered James the use

164

of the house. Do you have some rig running, Anthony?" his mama asked.

"Nothing you would want to know about, Mama."

"Tell me after it is over, and only tell me then if it turns out well. I am too tired to worry about your pranks. I had hoped you were going to settle down with Tess."

"I am merely cleaning the Augean stables in preparation for it," he replied obscurely.

Revel went to his room immediately after dinner. He took a small blue box from the dresser, opened it, and admired the diamond bracelet nestled within. Then he put the box in his pocket, went belowstairs, and asked Figgs to call his carriage.

"Don't we look dandy," Figgs said, running his eyes over Revel's toilette. "Must be a new lady."

"Do I not always look dandy. Figgs?"

"To be fair, you do, but you don't always have a box of diamonds in your pocket. I expect the set that was in your room are tucked in there," he said, reaching to see if he was right.

Revel gave his fingers a playful slap. "Don't tell Mama."

"Me lips might be sealed for a quid."

"Crook!" Revel laughed and tossed him a golden boy.

He went out and directed his carriage to Bridewell Lane.

Chapter Eighteen

Mrs. Marchant figured the bracelet would arrive by six, to pave the way for her husband's return. Six o'clock came and went, and still no parcel. The impatient lady was forced to the conclusion that Lyle was bringing it himself that evening—or he had not bought it at all. Perhaps he was not coming? Dinner might as well have been served in church, so far as conversation went, nor did the mood improve after dinner, when still the door knocker was silent.

When Mrs. Marchant was beyond speech, her daughters knew the situation was perilous, bordering on the irreparable. Before long, the dame's patience was at an end. She rose and said, "I shall be in my room, lying down with a migraine. If anyone calls, pray tell him I cannot receive visitors tonight."

"Yes, Mama," Tess said.

"I am sorry, Mama," Dulcie added, with a woeful face.

The girls remained in the saloon, sunk in gloomy silence, watching the blue-and-orange flames leap in the grate. Odd how such leaping flames brought no warmth. Tess felt frozen through to the marrow of her bones.

"If Papa does not come tonight," Dulcie said, "he might as well never come. She won't take him back. I know it. And it is all because of that stupid bracelet."

Tess, searching her conscience, could assure herself that at least the bracelet was not her fault. Yet she did feel culpable for adding to her mama's troubles recently, and wanted to expiate her sins.

"If only we could get the bracelet back, and give it to Papa to give Mama . . . It is intolerable that a stupid piece of stone and metal is tearing the family apart. We must get it back, somehow, Dulcie."

"But how? I wager Papa asked Mrs. Gardener for it already, and she refused."

"Brazen hussy! I have a good mind to go over and demand it."

"Would you really?" Dulcie asked, her eyes large with admiration. "You are so brave, Tess. I remember how you went to Lady Revel and asked her to make Lord James stop seeing Mama. You have such bottom."

Tess's threat had been an exaggeration, but when Dulcie looked at her with hope shining in her eyes, Tess began to wonder if the thing was not possible. Mrs. Gardener was a woman, after all. She had been a wife; she must have some tender feelings for family life.

"Yes, I would—really!" Tess said as her resolve firmed to determination. "But you must not tell Mama I have gone. I shall sneak out."

"How will you get to her apartment?"

"Bother, I'll need the carriage. We must take Crimshaw into our confidence."

Crimshaw was an old ally in family problems. He was the family butler from Northbay. As he was a high stickler in matters of deportment, however, Tess prevaricated to the extent of telling him she was calling on Lady Revel, to make up a fourth at whist. This, while unusual, was at least respectable, and he called for the carriage without argument.

Tess was trembling from head to foot when she climbed into the carriage and headed to Bridewell Lane. She knew which block of flats her quarry lived in, and would have only to read the nameplates to find the proper set of rooms. Her greatest fear was that Revel would be there. What would she say to him? The fear gradually turned to a sort of unripened hope as she envisaged the scene to come. She had inherited that much from her mama; the seed of the melodramatic was buried deep in her bosom.

You have Lord Revel, she would tell Mrs. Gardener, while smoting Revel with tear-filled eyes. Can you not give us back our father? Have you no womanly compassion? Do stones and metal mean more to you than our happiness?

Lord James was the first caller to arrive at Bridewell Lane and was entirely welcome. Mrs. Gardener, who had a keen understanding of gentlemen, was expecting him and had prepared an exquisite at-home toilette. Her first choice of black lace was rejected as being too racy. That Lord James did not know she was expecting him allowed her some latitude with regard to her outfit, but she did not want to appear obvious. The final choice was a flowing gown of creamy silk, embellished with much lace and many ribbons, and cut low to display her shoulders. Her raven hair was undressed and fell in languid waves about her cheeks as she curled up on the sofa with a novel.

She looked up with a question on her face when he was announced. "Lord James Drake? Do I have the pleasure of your acquaintance, sir?" she asked, with polite indifference, while her eyes assessed his appearance. A little old! But a good figure, and excellent tailoring. Then he smiled, and the years fell from him.

"Mrs. Gardener! You will think me the most farouche creature in all of Bath. Pray forgive my barging in unannounced."

"You catch me all unawares, sir! I am not dressed for company." She shrugged an apology, sending her gown an inch lower and revealing the swell of a satiny bosom. "May I ask what is the reason . . . ?"

James thrilled at her performance. Here was a lady who knew how to entice. "My nephew, Lord Revel, suggested I call on you when you go to London, but neglected to give me your address. As I was passing by, I thought I would drop off and discover it now. I shan't stay a moment, I promise you."

"Oh, I am not busy," she said hastily. "Just having a glance at a novel by Scott. Do stay and have a glass of wine." James was not tardy to slide a chair toward the sofa. "Yes, Revel mentioned his uncle was going to town."

She rose and went to get the wine—and show him her elegant figure. Lord James was bowled over. All this gorgeous femininity and twenty thousand besides!

"I should have offered to do that for you, Mrs. Gardener," he said, and darted to her side.

She peered up at him from beneath a sweep of

sable lashes and smiled. Such manners! Breeding always tells in the end. "Claret, port, brandy?" she asked.

"Claret is for boys. I'll have a man's drink, brandy."

"I thought you might," she said, with an alluring smile.

When they returned to the grate, Lord James abandoned the chair and sat beside her, where he spoke possessively of the Drake family house on Berkeley Square, where he would be staying in London. Did Mrs. Gardener care for the theater? She must be kind to an old bachelor and accompany him to the theater one evening. He had a season's ticket. Loved the theater—or perhaps it was just a lonely bachelor's way of passing an empty evening.

"Ah, I know what you mean, Lord James. Since Mr. Gardener's passing, I, too, have found the evenings long. But a good book is like a friend, in a way." She carefully arranged her skirt over the racy French novel that had been befriending her that evening.

Lord James was just rising to fetch the brandy bottle when there was a knock at the front door. Esmée looked at him in some alarm. "That may be Lord Revel, come to take his leave of me," she said. And to give me my diamond bracelet, in lieu of Marchant's trinket, she added to herself. It was vital that Lord James not be aware of that transaction.

She was vastly relieved when Lord James said, "You two old friends will want a moment alone."

"Must you leave?" she asked, to lend a casual touch to Revel's call.

James looked, trying to read her wishes. "I must

dash off a note to my man of business. Is there a study . . . ?"

"Across the hall, the end of the corridor. I shan't let him stay long." She was enjoying Lord James's call and had no aversion to prolonging it, as long as he remained unaware of the reason for Revel's call.

Lord James scuttled out, for he had assured Revel he would leave Bath that day. The possibility also existed that conversation might turn to the Revel family mansion on Berkeley Square—and its alias as the Drake mansion be revealed. Best to keep out of sight.

"Mr. Marchant," the butler announced, throwing Mrs. Gardener into a tizzy. What was that old fool doing here?

Mr. Marchant stepped in, wearing an angry scowl. "I know you are wishing me at Jericho, Esmée, but I really must ask you to return the bracelet. You have resumed relations with young Revel after all."

She glanced into the hallway, trying to decide whether Lord James could hear. "Pray lower your voice, Lyle," she said.

"I don't care who hears me. You have no right to keep the trinket if you are giving me my congé."

Here was a problem. Lord Revel was to give her the replacement bracelet in exchange for Marchant's. Revel might suspect trickery and not oblige her with the replacement. "I don't have it at the moment."

"What the deuce did you do with it? Have you hawked it already? I see how little it meant to you."

"No, no. You misunderstand, Lyle. The clasp was loose. I took it back to the jewelry store."

171

"Demme, I need it tonight. Lou will not have me back without it."

Esmée bit her lip and did some rapid mental conjuring. Revel could easily enough check her story and confirm that she had given the bracelet back to Marchant. She was most eager to be rid of Marchant, and giving him the demmed bracelet was the likeliest way of accomplishing it. She made a little moue. "Oh, very well," she said, laughing. "Just let me speak to my dresser. Perhaps she has not returned it yet."

She whisked out of the room and down to her bedchamber.

She was no sooner out of the saloon than the door knocker sounded again. Marchant was not slow to recognize the hated accents of Lord Revel. "Mrs. Gardener is expecting me, I believe."

"Certainly, milord."

Marchant had five seconds in which to consider the situation and make his decision. His dislike of Revel ran deep. What he really wanted to do was strike him, but as a duel at this time was really more than he could handle, he at least did not want to be disgraced in front of the man. Rushed into folly by the advancing footsteps, Marchant ran behind the sofa and hid. He knew as soon as he had done it that it was foolish, but to suddenly rise and make his presence known seemed even worse. He consoled himself that Esmée would realize he was there and make short shrift of Revel.

Esmée returned in half a minute, carrying the bracelet. "Revel." She smiled, looking around for Marchant, and was astonished to see no sign of him. She could only conclude he had heard Revel's carriage approach, peeked out the window and identified it, and left. Which was all to the good.

"You are punctual, sir!" She spotted Lord James's glass and quickly filled it up, before Revel saw it had been used. She handed it to him. "A quick drink, before you have to leave?"

"What, pushing me out the door before I have delivered the goods, Esmée?" he asked.

"You are not a minute too soon, Revel." She laughed. "Marchant was just here, demanding his bracelet."

"The devil you say! Did you give it to him?"

"I had just gone to get it. Here," she said, handing it to him. "You'll see he gets it?"

"I shall go directly to the Pelican from here."

Marchant listened, trying to make sense of it. Revel was going to give the bracelet to him? Why would he do that?

Mrs. Gardener obligingly asked, "You are going to a great deal of trouble on his behalf. I daresay it has something to do with Miss Marchant?"

"But of course. I am trying to get her parents together, to show her how effectual I am."

"Then are we to assume you are finally caught in the parson's mousetrap?" Esmée asked.

"It looks that way," he replied, "if the lady will have me."

Mr. Marchant could hardly contain his delight. Revel marrying Tess! By Jove, wait till he told Lou this! She would welcome him with open arms when he ran this news to her. It was better than the diamond bracelet. Tess! Who would have thought it? Revel must be mad.

Mrs. Gardener thought the same thing, but her primary concern at that moment was Lord James, cooling his heels in her study. She wished to speed Revel's departure. "Aren't you forgetting something?" she asked coyly.

He reached into his jacket pocket and drew out the blue box. "Are you, by any chance, referring to this?" he asked.

She snatched the box and opened it. Her practiced eye soon recognized the superiority of the stones. She drew it out and tried to fasten it around her wrist. "Very nice, Revel. What lovely diamonds. Can you help me? I am all thumbs."

This caused Marchant a moment's pause. Revel giving Esmée diamonds when he was on the verge of offering for Tess? He was ready to take offense, until it occurred to him it was Revel's farewell gift to Esmée. Very generous of him. What need had Esmée for a second bracelet, at such a time?

There was yet another knock at the front door. Revel looked up and smiled. James! He had an inkling he would not wait until Esmée got to London. Esmée could not think of anyone else of any importance who might be calling. It must be someone begging money for some charity.

Lord Revel reached forward and fumbled with the catch of the bracelet. When it was secured, he held her wrist up and admired it. "You do the trinket proud, Esmée," he said, and kissed her fingers in a gallant gesture.

He glanced to the doorway to see who the butler was showing in. His eyes grew large and he dropped Esmée's hand. "Tess!" he exclaimed.

Chapter Nineteen

All Tess's rehearsed lines flew out of her head at the sight before her. Revel, not only comfortably ensconced in Esmée's saloon, but actually kissing her. Tess's throat felt as if it had caved in, preventing speech, and even breathing. Not so much as a strangled gasp escaped her lips. She just stood as though turned to stone, incapable of moving, while her heart crumbled to dust within her.

Until that moment, she had not really believed Revel had returned to Esmée. Oh, her mind grasped the fact, but her heart had never believed it.

Revel and Esmée seemed to be struck down with the same paralysis. The three remained perfectly immobile, staring at one another for what seemed a brief eternity, but was, in fact, thirty seconds. It was long enough for Tess to recognize Revel's expression as guilt, rapidly changing to anger.

It was Esmée who recovered first. She withdrew her hand from Revel's, gave his chin a playful tap, and said to Tess, "I believe it is Miss Marchant, is it not? Do come in, Miss Marchant." The diamonds at Esmée's wrist caught the light and scattered tiny rainbows in the air.

Tess pulled her eyes from the diamond bracelet and turned them to Revel. He had regained his sangfroid and forced a welcoming smile on his handsome face. Astonishment robbed him of his manners, however, and he forgot to rise. "Tess! What brings you here?" he asked in a strange voice.

After a few inaudible attempts, Tess finally forced out a speech, uttered in some stranger's voice. "I came to see Mrs. Gardener, but I see she is busy. Pray, do not let me interrupt you." She turned on her heel and fled the room, before her tears spurted. She would not cry in front of him!

Revel was suddenly galvanized into action. He jumped from the sofa and went after her. He caught her just as she was rushing to the front door. "Tess, don't be an idiot!" he said.

She turned on him, fire sparking from her eyes. "Don't you call me an idiot again!"

He raised his hands as though to ward off a blow. "It was just a manner of speech."

"I don't care for your manner of speech, sir, or for your manner of—of anything else!"

"Why did you come?" he asked. "You must have known I would be here."

"I am not a mind reader. And don't think I came in hopes of seeing you, because I did not."

Their voices were perfectly audible to Esmée, who listened in amusement. Mr. Marchant also heard, and was overcome with a dreadful fear that Tess was about to lose her coronet. When Esmée rose and went into the hall, he peered above the sofa, contemplating how he could nudge Tess into line without revealing his presence. He saw his diamond bracelet on the sofa table and put it in his pocket while he had the opportunity.

Esmée said, "Miss Marchant, pray do not run

away. Come and have a glass of wine." She took Tess's elbow to lead her back to the saloon.

The bracelet glittered enticingly, reminding Tess why she had come. Her eye was not so well trained in diamonds as her hostess's. She mistook it for what she considered her mama's bracelet. Her life might be ruined, but maybe she could yet pull one little victory from the ashes. Esmée would not wish to appear grasping in front of her new lover. Tess let herself be returned to the saloon, and even accepted a glass of wine—with all the enthusiasm of Socrates accepting the glass of hemlock.

After a sustaining sip, she said, "I came to ask you if you would give me the bracelet Papa gave you. Mama will not have him back without it, you see, and as you have—have taken a new lover—"

"Tess!" Revel said in an admonishing tone, for there was no counting on Esmée to remain a lady in the face of such wanton provocation as this.

Esmée was kept in humor by her coming trip to London and the intriguing Lord James. She just gave Tess a blighting stare, then glanced to the table and noticed the bracelet was missing. She assumed Revel had taken it and replied, "You are mistaken, Miss Marchant. I do not take lovers. Your papa and I were platonic friends. When you are a little older, you will realize that such a thing is indeed possible. Your papa did not give me a diamond bracelet."

Tess stared pointedly at her sparkling wrist and said, "I see," in a tone of heavy sarcasm.

"You refer, I think, to the bracelet I helped your papa select for his wife." Behind the sofa, Mr. Marchant smiled softly and listened while Esmée spoke on. "He left it here, as he did not wish to leave it

177

at the inn, for fear of a robbery. Revel dropped by this evening to pick it up for him."

"For Papa?" Tess asked. She had a pretty sound idea she was being conned—and wished to reveal Esmée as a liar.

"That's right. Show her the bracelet, Revel, for if I am not mistaken, Miss Marchant thinks this one I am wearing is her mama's bracelet."

Revel looked to the table. Esmée did the same. They looked a question at each other, then both began scrabbling around the wineglasses and bibelots scattered on the table's surface. "It's gone!" Esmée exclaimed.

"How very strange!" Tess said triumphantly.

Marchant was on thorns to return the trinket to its rightful place, but could see no way of doing it without revealing his presence.

"It must have fallen," Revel said, and leaned down to peer under the sofa, then around at the side. Marchant, seeing his chance, held out his arm and dangled the bracelet in the air. Revel, seeing only a disembodied arm, immediately suspected James. What series of events had pitched him behind the sofa was still to be discovered, but whatever rig James was running, there was no point in embarrassing him in front of Miss Marchant.

He took the bracelet and said, "Here it is. It must have fallen, as I said."

"There you are then," Esmée said. "Give it to Miss Marchant, Revel, as she is so eager to have it."

Tess accepted it and put it in her reticule, while trying to think of some smart retort for Esmée's insinuating charge.

Revel could foresee nothing but disaster from

prolonging the visit. "I shall take you home, Tess," he said, and reached for her hand.

"Let Miss Marchant finish her wine, Revel," Esmée said. "You will give her the idea she is not welcome."

"I would not dream of taking you away, Lord Revel," Tess said coldly. "I have the carriage waiting."

"I was just about to leave," he insisted. "I only came to pick up your mama's bracelet. We shall take it to Mr. Marchant, at the Pelican."

Marchant smiled in satisfaction. That was a close call, but things were working out nicely. As soon as they left, he'd run out into the street and grab a hansom cab to take him to the Pelican.

No sounds had penetrated to the study for some fifteen minutes now. Lord James wondered if Revel had left yet. He had thought Esmée would call him, but perhaps she was lending credence to the polite fiction that he had letters to write and was not going to disturb him. Surely it would not take Revel more than fifteen minutes to say good-bye. James was eager to get back to the widow. He quietly opened the door and cocked his ear toward the saloon, heard nothing, and took a few steps forward.

"There is no need for us both to go. I shall take it," Tess said firmly.

Hearing the echo of Tess Marchant's voice, Lord James became extremely curious. He tiptoed forward, hoping for a quick peek before darting back to the study. One peek was all it took for Tess to spot him.

"Lord James!" she exclaimed.

"Good evening," he said. Forced to put a good complexion on his appearance, he entered and bowed to the group, then turned to Esmée. "Mrs. Gardener. I see Revel is here, so I shall not have to introduce myself. He suggested I call on you before leaving for London. I hear you are about to go there, too."

Tess heard this with delight. She looked to Revel, planning to honor him with a smile, but he was paying her no heed. Revel looked from Lord James to the sofa. How had he done that? Was the man a magician? Revel looked behind the sofa and found himself staring into the beleaguered face of Mr. Marchant. Marchant lifted a finger to his lips, pleading for silence. Revel controlled his vocal organs, but his body gave an uncontrolled leap and his face looked as if he had seen a ghost. Soon Esmée and Tess went to have a look.

"Mr. Marchant!"

"Papa!"

Marchant rose and smiled all around. "I cannot find it, Esmée," he said, frowning in perplexity, then explained to the others. "I have been searching on hands and knees for the crown of my watch. It fell off when I was winding my timepiece, and rolled under the sofa. Perhaps your servant will come across it when she is sweeping, Esmée. Well, well. I see quite a little party has collected while I have been searching. Tess, Lord James, Revel." He bowed to each in turn.

"Papa!" Tess exclaimed. "What on earth are you doing here?"

"Did I not just say I was looking for my crown?"

"Yes, but—"

Revel took pity on the man and cut Tess off in midspeech. "Let us all have a look for it," he suggested.

"Never mind," Marchant said. "The jeweler can replace it, I daresay."

Lord James recognized a havey-cavey situation when he stumbled into one and threw his mite in to salvage the affair. "Quite a little party," he said, happy to divert attention from his own magical appearance. He would wait until the others had left before asking Esmée what the devil was going on.

"I did not hear you come in, James," Revel said.

"Did you not? With two ladies to entertain, it is not to be wondered at. I just arrived. The butler was busy, and I did not have myself announced."

"Lord James is going to call on me in London," Esmée said, unwittingly revealing that she had already had words with him.

Revel and James exchanged an amused look.

Marchant drew out his watch and said, "Well, it is getting pretty late." When he noticed the crown in place, to give the lie to his tale, he covered it with his thumb, but not before Revel's sharp eyes had seen it.

"Indeed it is. We shall leave you in peace now, Mrs. Gardener," Revel said. "I wish you every happiness in London. And you, James," he added, with a lifted brow.

"Do drop in when you are in town, Revel," James said. "Always room for one more at Berkeley Square."

"Not for long, though," Revel said, but he said it in a low voice and with a smile.

Mrs. Gardener went to the door to speed the three parting guests.

It was a clear, cold night. Moonlight silvered the cobblestones and a cutting wind blew a few stray snowflakes through the still air.

"Thank God you have the carriage, Tess," Marchant said. "You have the bracelet?"

She handed it to him. "You have some explaining to do, Papa," she said.

"Not in this filthy wind. Meet us at the Pelican, Revel. Or will you go with Revel, Tess?"

"I shall go with you, Papa," she said, and marched to their carriage. "Papa, what were you doing there?" she demanded as soon as they were alone.

"Why, I went to get your mama's bracelet, to be sure, same as you, Tess. What should I be doing at Mrs. Gardener's?"

"Revel said *he* went to pick up the bracelet."

Invention was not yet at an end. Marchant searched his mind and said, "He was to go with me, in case your mama did not like my going alone, but he was late. I was so eager to have the matter sewn up that I went along without him."

"It seems very strange," she said, dissatisfied.

"What seems a deal stranger to me, miss, is your going to such a house. That was completely uncalled for."

"If you had to live at Bartlett Street with Mama in the boughs you would not ask why I went."

"How is she?" he asked in a softer voice.

"How do you think she would be, when you have been carrying on with that woman? This must stop, Papa. She has had more than enough of your chasing after lightskirts. If it happens again, she shan't have you back. She really means it this time. You have hurt her very badly, and Dulcie, too. And me, Papa," she added, with a wounded look.

"It won't happen again, my dear. I am through with all that. You'll see. And now let us speak of your future, my dear. You have done pretty well, nabbing young Revel."

"I have not nabbed him, and don't you *dare* suggest to him that he must marry me."

"I suggest it? Did I not hear him with my own ears tell Esmée he plans to marry you, if you'll have him?"

"Did he say that?" Tess asked in a trembling voice.

"I heard him plain as day, when I was—*harumph*—looking for my crown. Found it in my pocket, after all that searching. Heh, heh."

Tess's bemused state let him get away with that awful plumper. They met Revel at the Pelican, but there no longer seemed any necessity to go inside. Reconciling with his wife was more important to Lyle than packing up his belongings and paying the reckoning. He would do that tomorrow. They decided to drive directly to Bartlett Street.

Marchant said, "Just leave me alone in the carriage, Tess, so that I may work up a pretty little speech to make to your mama. You can go with Lord Revel."

"We'll give you some time alone before we go in," Revel said.

He directed his groom to drive west, toward the Crescent Gardens. While they drove through the city, Revel said, "There was something very strange about that visit to Esmée's. I felt I had fallen into a French farce, with people popping out from nowhere. I fully expected a screen to fall over, revealing your mama and Dulcie."

"Except there was not any screen. Did Papa ask you to go with him?"

"I had no idea he was going. Nor that he was

there, hiding behind the sofa. What can account for it? And James . . . Where the deuce did *he* pop up from?"

"He did not come in at the front door. He came from the other end of the hall."

Revel automatically assumed James came from the bedchamber and was impressed with his uncle's celerity. "Powdering his nose, perhaps," he said facetiously.

"Papa said you and he were to go to Esmée's together, but you were late, so he went on alone. I do think he went to ask Esmée for the bracelet, though. I shan't pester him with questions. I think he really means to reform this time."

"And if he does not, I shan't pull his chestnuts from the fire again. Let him smoke in the private little hell of his own devising."

"What do you mean, *you* shan't pull his chestnuts from the fire? I don't see why it was necessary for you to be asking favors of Esmée. Why were you there, Revel, if Papa did not ask you to go?" She gasped as realization dawned. "You were putting a diamond bracelet on her wrist when I came in! You gave it to her!"

"So you noticed that. I thought as much. You were looking hard enough. And you think I gave it to her. Actually, I did, but—"

"You, too! Oh, really, Revel. You are as bad as Papa!"

"My dear idiot!"

"Don't call me an idiot again!"

"You *are* an idiot, if you think what you are thinking . . . I mean what I think you are thinking."

"A lady is not given diamonds for no reason," she said angrily.

"I had a very good reason . . . to get your papa's bracelet back. I bought it for an exchange."

"But why should *you* pay?"

"Because, dear genius, your papa's pockets were to let, and I wanted to have the matter finished."

"Why were you kissing her wrist?"

"Because it was there." Her chin thrust forward in annoyance. "So were her lips, but I was not kissing them," he pointed out.

"It was all a hum that she would not take gifts from her patrons."

"Perhaps she felt that accepting the bracelet would nudge your father into a proposal. Or perhaps she just decided her standards were too high. I daresay standards do tend to lower as a lady's age rises."

"It certainly looked as if you were making up to her," Tess said, unconvinced by his speech.

"How can you think I was making up to Esmée when I am in love with you?" he said angrily.

The declaration robbed her of argument. She looked shyly at him, and said in a thrushlike voice her mama would have approved, "Are you really, Revel?"

"I must be. I can't eat; I can't sleep. I keep seeing you at Revel Hall, at the foot of my table, scolding me. It must be love."

"It sounds more like the megrims," she said doubtfully. Yet similar sensations had been bedeviling her, and she knew she was hopelessly in love with Revel.

"There is only one way to be sure," he said, pulling her into his arms. By the wan moonlight, he gazed at her upturned face a long moment before lowering his lips to kiss her. How had he lived next door to Tess for decades without realizing she was

185

the perfect wife for him? It shone forth now, blinding him with its inevitability.

His heart swelled, and he was suffused with a golden rush of tenderness as the kiss deepened. He knew he had found something precious, something too rare and valuable to risk by any future dalliance with lightskirts. How could men be such savages as to hurt the thing they loved and cherished?

He kissed her long and passionately, as if he would never let her go.

Oh, yes, it was surely love. When a man took the idiotic notion life was not worth living without that one special person, he was in love. Eventually he lifted his head and gazed at her, while a bemused smile tugged at his lips. "Well, I think that settles it. *I* certainly hear bells ringing," he said softly. "The music of the spheres."

"It's the night watch, actually," she said. Echoes of "Ten of the clock, and all's well" came through the window.

"That is one of the many things I love about you, Tess Marchant. You always keep one foot firmly planted on the earth," he said in a voice choked with emotion.

"Do I?" she asked from the comfort of his shoulder. "How very odd. I feel as though I am floating on air."

"We call it cloud nine," he said, and kissed her again.

At Bartlett Street, the Marchants were also on cloud nine. "You did not have to do that, Lyle," Lou said, locking the diamond bracelet on to her wrist. "Good gracious, as though I cared about a silly old bracelet. It was just your giving it to her that hurt me."

"Giving diamonds to Esmée Gardener? Nothing of the sort. She just helped me select the thing."

"You already knew which one I wanted, dear," she reminded her beloved.

"Oh, very well then, there was another reason. Esmée has an in with the fellow who runs the shop. She told me she could get a discount."

This was a perfectly feasible excuse and was not questioned further, except for, "How much discount?"

"Ten percent," he lied promptly.

"Why did you give it to her in the Pump Room? Admit you did that to make me jealous."

"Fair is fair, Lou. I was jealous as a green cow about Lord James. He has taken up with Mrs. Gardener, by the by."

"You never mean it! Now there is a perfect pair. They will lead each other a merry chase."

"Serves them right," he said severely. "Isn't it about time Revel was bringing Tess home?"

"If it is to be a match, he may keep her out till midnight tonight, with my blessing, for he knows I have always been a very strict mother in the past. You may be sure that had a deal to do with his offering for her. Those rakes always choose a well-behaved lady when it comes to marriage. Imagine, Lyle. Tess a countess." She clapped her hands in delight.

"Dulcie will be a duchess, certainly."

"And Tess was courted in Bath, like me. There is romance in the air in this town, I swear."

Marchant thought silence the best reply to that troublesome speech.

Soon Revel and Tess entered, wearing the telltale smiles of two people in love. Revel's asking Marchant for his daughter's hand was a mere formality. The gentlemen had more interesting things to discuss. The whoops of laughter coming from the study as Marchant confessed his predicament behind the sofa were taken for paternal joy by the fond mama, and went unheard by Tess, who had soared in her mind to cloud nine, where she was above mere mortal considerations.

At Bridewell Lane, Lord James was also making headway with his inamorata. "Sorry I stumbled in on that fracas," he said. "I was beginning to think you had forgotten all about me."

"Forget you, Lord James?" she asked, smiling tenderly. "I thought they would never leave. But we are alone now." Her dark eyes looked an invitation.

"I did not mean to stay so long, on the first call. I ought to be running along, too. I daresay Revel can put me up for the night. I have given up my room at the hotel." He peered hopefully at Esmée for her reaction.

She smiled softly. "It is only ten o'clock. Have another drink, and keep me company awhile."

She poured her brandy. Neither of them had any intention of Lord James sleeping anywhere but at Bridewell Lane. What did she care what a bunch of Bath quizzes thought of her now, when she was about to take London? Lord James was worried about how he would later explain having to leave the family mansion on Berkeley Square. Esmée, who knew perfectly well who owned the house, was only concerned to be married from that prestigious address and launch her career amid the ton with one fine party.

"Just a small one then," James said, and allowed her to fill his glass.